CW00867071

Sarah's Story

Sarah's Story

Helen Susan Swift

For
my one love

Prelude

'To lose one husband is unfortunate,' Kitty said severely, 'but to lose two is careless. I certainly hope that you can retain husband number three a little bit longer, Sarah.' She gave a melodramatic sigh. 'I have never known a woman experience so many misadventures in affairs of the heart.'

I was not quite sure how to respond to that, so I showed her a cold shoulder. I always found that the best way to respond to Kitty Chillerton when she is being hurtful.

'You can't ignore me, Sarah Bembridge,' Kitty said, as we walked toward Knighton Hazard with the rolling fields stretching away on either side and a light rain drifting in from the Channel half a mile ahead.

She was right of course. Kitty was always the most irritating of women and so very hard to ignore, much as I wanted to.

'You had better try and make this marriage last longer,' Kitty continued. 'You already have a reputation as a harbinger of misfortune.'

Ouch. That one stung, probably because there was a lot of truth in it. I took a deep breath and looked toward Knighton Hazard and its chapel that seemed fated to be the nemesis of my misfortunes. I had a sudden feeling of sick despair as I remembered what had happened on my previous two visits here as an eager young bride, and then I had a moment of inspiration. You must have had them, these flashes of realisation where you suddenly see something that should have been obvious days or months ago.

I stopped exactly where I was, nearly upsetting Kitty onto the ground, which is nothing more than she deserved, the dragon-tongued hussy. 'Good Lord,' I said, which was very mild when one considers what I had been through the last few months.

'Good Lord what?' Kitty asked, somewhat fretfully. 'Oh do come along, Sarah; have you forgotten that we have a wedding to prepare for? Or perhaps you have already decided to discard husband number three and are contemplating husband number four?'

'Good Lord,' I repeated, partly because I was not quite certain if I could perform the necessary act, and partly to further irritate Kitty. She was my dearest and most amiable companion, you see, and a woman does not hate or love anybody quite as much as her closest female friend.

'What is it that ails you so?' Kitty pushed me in her agitation. 'Would you stop Good Lording and pray tell me?'

'I had an idea that may remove the ill luck from my weddings,' I said, blithely aware that I was further stretching Kitty's inquisitiveness. It is a well-known saying that curiosity killed the Kitty. Well, I had no intentions of ending poor Kitty's life, irritating though she was, but I had no qualms about torturing her imagination.

'So tell me!' She stamped her foot in petulance which, you may imagine, pleased me no end.

'I shall take them down!' I announced, as if I had discovered a way of terminating Bonaparte's threat to the world once and for all. 'And that will put an end to it.'

'You shall take what down?' Kitty wailed in utter frustration, and so I told her. But if I told you at this juncture, then I should have begun near the end of my tale, and that is wrong-headed. All tales should begin at the beginning, and that is exactly what I shall do now, so please bear with me while I go back a few months when I was a frivolous and empty headed young girl and not the intelligent and mature woman I am now.

Chapter One

There was a fog the night he arrived. It rolled in from the Channel, cold and clammy as it clung to the curves of the cove and crept up the flanks of St Catherine's Chine toward our home. Sitting at the corner seat at my bedroom window, I watched its slow progress, as the white fingers feathered past the ancient oak and the Watching Rock where the smugglers sat to spy on the Excisemen, slithered onto the Down and frittered around the neatly clipped hedgerow boundary of our garden.

When the advance tendrils reached the chalk clunch walls of our house I hurriedly pulled shut the window and locked it tight. I don't like fog; I never have and I never will, except for one occasion that I will come to by-and-by. It is uncanny the manner in which it hides things and distorts shapes so trees can appear like people and horses like the strange monsters from children's stories. I like things open and honest and straight. Bad things happen in the fog; it is the home of smugglers and Frenchmen and Excisemen, all of which should be avoided. Except maybe the smugglers; the gentlemen of the night are useful when we need more French brandy for the wine cellars, or ribbons for my hair.

But that night I shut out the fog and hoped it would stay away.

Baffled in its attempts to invade out home, the fog recoiled and shifted in-land, to spread out and smother all the landmarks of St Catherine's Down and northward to the bulk of the Island. We live on Wight, you see, that great, diamond shaped island on the south of England, Eden's Garden, the fairest place in the world, but exposed to the mists and storms of the Channel on the times when the weather is foul. Now please pay attention while I give a brief lesson in geography to those of lesser knowledge than you. I will not be asking questions but it may make my little story easier to understand.

All right then: we live in the Horse Head Inn, which is situated on the south coast of Wight, just a seagull's cry from St Catherine's Point, the most southerly tip of the island. It nestles under a ridge of St Catherine's Down, yet is still open to the Channel weather in all its variety from biting winds to ugly fogs. My mother runs this inn and has done ever since the French captured my father at sea five years back and we had to rely entirely on our own resources. We look south and ever south to where the great ocean stretches to the coast of France and beyond to Spain and the broad Atlantic and the sugar islands of the West Indies, although of course the curve of the world and sheer distance precludes us from seeing these magical lands.

I shivered, altered my stance and peered out to sea for that day there was nothing. I could see nothing; where normally the Channel would be speckled with the riding lights of ships, the mist had erased all visibility as if by the sweep of a giant's hand. I thought of the poor seamen shivering out there with each vessel isolated by fog so it was a floating island in a hostile sea, prey to French privateers, the treacherous Channel tides or the press gangs of the Navy.

'Sarah!' The voice cracked into my reverie so I looked up. 'Sarah: come down here girl!'

I sighed, straightened my dress and obeyed, stomping hard on the bare wooden stairs to show my displeasure at being disturbed. The stairs led directly to the tap room where my mother was busy washing an array of pewter tankards. 'Yes, Mother? What is it?'

'It's going to be a thick night, Sarah; I don't think we'll be busy, so best take the opportunity to get the place clean.'

'Yes, Mother,' I said, making it obvious I resented the idea, while making sure I kept out of reach of my mother's ready hand. I should have known she would find some way of spoiling the night for me and she was obsessed with cleanliness. Who cared if there was an old leaf or a speck of seaweed underfoot? Sighing, I shifted the tables and chairs out of the way and began to brush the sanded floorboards. Mother watched for a moment, opened her mouth to find fault with something then closed it again and began to check the barrels. I sighed and continued.

The rumble shook the inn so the glasses rattled together and Mother looked up from her task.

'Thunder,' I said, taking any excuse as a distraction from cleaning. 'You were right Mother dear. It's going to be a wild night.' I smiled, prepared to be friendly again. I had learned that it was always best to keep on Mother's right side. I knew she was getting old you see; she must have been nearing forty then: quite in her dotage to my youthful eyes.

She looked up, said nothing and continued with whatever she was doing.

'God help sailors on a night like this,' I said. There was nothing false about that well-used statement. Living on the south coast of Wight or the Back of Wight as we term it, we were always aware of the fickle nature of the sea.

'God help them indeed,' Mother said softly. She stepped beside me and laid a hand on my shoulder. 'You get that floor finished Sarah, and then I want you to…' I never heard what her mother wanted next as a louder than average peal of thunder set the shutters trembling and echoed from the cliffs a few yards from the inn.

'Dear God in Heaven,' Mother said, and touched a hand to her heart. 'It's a perfect hurricane.'

By that time people had been entering the Horse Head, looking for ale to fortify them against the weather, or something stronger if they had a throat for spirits. My good friend Kitty seldom entered the inn, as she and Mother did not see eye-to-eye and young single women are not always comfortable in the company of the rough privateers, coastal sailors and free-traders who frequented this coast in these heady, dangerous days. There are always exceptions of course and in our case they are old Mrs Downer who saw all and heard all and says nothing, and Molly Draper, who would position herself in a corner and talk to anybody.

'Weather's getting a bit rough,' Molly agreed. She was one of the few friends who remained by me despite my inquisitive nature.

'Things could get busy later,' Mother said cryptically, and Molly smiled.

'There'll be pickings,' she said. I liked Molly. She was born on the wrong side of the blanket, and her father, so they said, was the Reverend Barwis. She was slightly older than me and once or twice took me to the church at Binstead, where there is a most scandalous ancient idol of a woman holding open her private person in the most outrageous fashion. All the local boys used to point and mock and make comments until their mothers discovered them and put such a flea in their ear that they would never forget. And quite right too.

Although I guessed what she meant I kept my own council, which was unusual for me.

'Sarah,' Mother called for me to serve the master of a Ventnor coaster who had put back into harbour due to the bad weather.

'We're due for a real pea-souper of a fog,' the master said. I knew him well, John Nash, a good man with a stout wife and six children.

'Well Captain Nash,' I said brightly, 'I am sure you are safe in here until it all blows over.'

'That won't be till the small hours,' John Nash said, 'I'll just have a couple and get back home.' He shifted himself comfortable on the wooden chair, sighed deeply and sunk a tankard of ale in a succession of mighty swallows that augured well for Mother's profits but ill for his waistline.

I settled my mind for a long night's work if there were others like John Nash looking for a quiet refreshment. I saw his wet boot prints on the floor and wondered why I had ever bothered sweeping up.

John Nash was correct about the weather. The fog thickened until the Horse Head seemed pressed down by the weight of it, seeped under the door and hovered at the windows until Mother ordered me outside to close the shutters and keep out the damp. I did so, and was surprised when Molly came to help.

She pumped me for information about our few customers and I told her in fervent whispers, with the great rollers crashing on the bay beneath us and the mist clinging to our hair and clothes. She had the strangest eyes, Molly, as if she could read inside your head and see what you were thinking, but she was the most amiable of companions.

'Wait...' Molly held up her hand, palm toward me. 'Something is happening.'

I stopped in mid-sentence. When Molly said that sort of thing it was best to take heed.

'Listen,' she took hold of my sleeve and stared out to sea.

I listened. At first I thought it was more thunder, the rolling sort that grumbles away for a long time and then fades into nothing without there being any lightning or even rain. I was wrong though, which was more usual than I cared to admit. It was not any sort of thunder.

'That's gunfire,' John Nash joined us outside. He lifted his tankard to indicate the south west. 'Coming from that way.'

'No,' I said, for of course I knew better than he did. 'It's from over there,' I pointed south east by east.

John Nash shook his head. 'The fog distorts sound,' he said, speaking serious-like and without his usual smile. 'It's south west by west; two vessels at least.' He pointed with his tankard again. 'See there?'

At first I saw nothing but the greasy coils of fog, shifting around the coast and hugging the beach like an ugly grey blanket.

'I see it,' Molly said and, not to be outdone, I chimed in.

'So do I.'

'What do you see?' Mother had joined us. She put both hands on my shoulder, either to ensure I did not fall over the cliff and lose her an unpaid skivvy or because she might actually care for me. Probably the former, I thought, uncharitably.

Then I did see it. Great white flashes through the fog, flickering a few seconds ahead of another of those deep rumbles. 'Lightning,' I said at once. It was in the south west, exactly where John Nash said and nowhere near where I thought.

'That is the muzzle flare of cannon,' John Nash said quietly. 'A broadside of six pounders I reckon, so maybe a brig of war or the like.' He took a swallow of his ale, 'or a Revenue cutter after a smuggler or mebbe a Frog privateer taking advantage of the fog to coast our shores and snap up a prize or two.'

'It's lucky you did not venture out, John,' Mother's grip tightened on my shoulders, as they often did when there was talk of trouble at sea.

'Aye, lucky,' John Nash said. He patted Mother's arm in a gesture I did not yet understand. 'He is a good man, Charlotte; a good man and he is missed. If the French still hold him they may exchange him soon.'

'Aye.' Mother touched his hand, and then altered her tone. 'Why is my counter not polished bright? It is ten minutes since I told you, Sarah! Come on girl, there is work to be done.'

'There is always work to be done,' I said, but rather than obey, I watched Mother as she peered out the open door. I joined her and we both stared into the white fog, holding each other close. I could feel her shivering.

'It's all right, Mother,' I said. I rubbed my hand up and down her back. I never knew what to say on these occasions.

'I was thinking of your father,' Mother said softly as if I did not know, and then straightened up. 'Oh well, Sarah. There is nothing we can do here. This is not getting the place tidy. Come on girl and get the work done.'

She slapped my arm for me but this time I felt no resentment. Mother had nearly let me inside her secret thoughts there. For one second she had opened up that hidden hurt and I was grateful to her for the confidence.

I finished the floor, starting every time the gunfire sounded, but after a while the noise stopped and our customers drifted away in a hubbub of noise and a reek of stale ale. Then there was nothing but the slow ticking of the grandfather clock that was my mother's pride and joy. It stood in the corner of the room diagonally opposite the door so it was the first thing that guests and customers saw when they walked in. It was a beautiful creation of honey oak with an arched face and Roman numerals that ticked softly.

'Don't just look at it then, Sarah,' Mother said. 'Polish it so it gleams.' As I did so, she stood behind me, ensuring I did the best job I possibly could.

'That was your father's wedding gift to me,' Mother told me as if I could ever forget. 'He ordered it specially made from Richard Clarke of Newport and used all the prize money from three years voyaging to buy it and he will want to see it pristine when he walks in the door.'

I nodded as I applied the beeswax and polished away for dear life. One has always to work one's hardest when Mother is around.

'He will come back soon now,' mother said, 'you can depend on it.'

'Yes Mother,' I agreed. The oak was a fine sheen now, gleaming so it reflected my face in the body of the clock.

Mother looked up and jerked her thumb toward the door. 'I heard hoof beats, so there will be another guest.'

How did she do that? How could she hear so much? I had heard nothing but if Mother said she had heard a horse, then a horse she had heard. Sure enough, only a few moments later the door opened and a stranger walked in. My life started anew, although I did not know that yet. At that minute he was only an anonymous guest coming to disturb my peace and help us square the accounts, but soon that man would be the centrepiece of all sorts of troubles. A billow of mist followed him like smoke around the tail of Beelzebub; it dissipated the moment he slammed shut the door yet it was that image that remains in my mind even yet as I remember that moment; the stranger that life had used hard with the mist coiling like smoke in his wake. I looked at him as he surveyed the room, noting his weather-battered appearance and the deep tan of his face. He looked like the mate of a merchant vessel or perhaps the master of a coasting brig, but down on his luck to judge by the threadbare clothes he wore. Yet even then I knew there was more; there was a presence about this man that I had never met before.

'Is this the Horse Head Inn?' The man asked. His voice was so sharp edged it could have chopped through an oaken plank, but there was an intonation in it that I did not recognise. He certainly was not a Caulkhead, a native of the island; he was an Overner, a mainlander but so obviously a seaman that I could forgive him his origin. I imagined him roaring his lungs out at the height of a Channel gale and wondered if my father was of his ilk. I pushed that thought away as well; I had no desire to court sorrow.

'It is the Horse Head Inn,' I agreed. I wondered if I should mention the sign board that swung above the front door, with the name proudly displayed.

"Then I have come to the right place." The man removed his tricorne hat and placed it on the counter that doubled as a work desk. I ignored the moisture that ran onto the wood that I had bees-waxed with much labour only that morning, but noticed the deep cut on the hat that had been roughly cobbled together. The stitching was hurried, rough; it was the handiwork of a man but I wondered what had caused that slash. It matched the less-than-subtle patch that had been placed on the sleeve of his travelling cloak and the black paint that tried hard to disguise the scuffed leather of the riding boots. His clothes had seen hard wear indeed, augmented by a hard life, I suspected. Helping my mother run an inn gave me much insight into people.

'I want a room for a week, to begin with,' the man said.

My mother dried her hands and arms on a rag as she moved closer from her position at the wash tub. She eyed the man up and down, her eyes narrow. 'We always ask an *arenest* here,' she said, and quickly translated from Wight talk into mainland English for the benefit of the Overner. 'We ask for a sum to bind the bargain in advance.'

I was not sure if the man was going to laugh or snarl, but he compromised with a small smile. 'And you shall have it,' he said.

Of course I knew why my mother was being so rude. We had bitter experience of Overner guests who arrived and demanded a room, only to leave a few days later without paying a brass farthing. We were wary of strangers with long pockets and short arms, especially in these hard times. All the same, I felt quite sorry for this seaman in his battered tricorne hat and coat that had obviously seen better days. More fool me, as it turned out, but I did not know him, then.

As the man reached inside his cloak, mother pressed her forefinger onto the counter. 'I wish your name as well, sir. I do not care for strangers who remain anonymous.'

'Howard.' The man said after a short but significant pause. 'Adam Howard.'

My mother grunted. 'So you say.' She had noticed that hesitation as well. She held out her right hand, palm uppermost. 'I charge five shillings a week Mr Howard, for board and lodgings.'

Mr Howard raised his eyebrows. 'Five shillings,' he repeated, in a tone that might have contained wonderment or amusement or both.

'In advance,' Mother insisted.

Mr Howard sighed and pulled out his pocketbook. He used his hand to shield the contents as he extracted a silver crown, but I heard the musical chink of coin on coin and knew he was not quite as purse-pinched as his appearance would suggest.

He placed the coin in mother's palm. 'Here are five shillings, Ma'am.'

Mother lifted the crown piece, bit into it to test the purity of the silver and placed it in the leather purse she wore tethered from the belt around her waist. 'Sarah will show you to your room, sir. You have baggage?'

I noticed the change in Mother's term of address from a terse 'Mr Howard' to a more respectful 'sir'. She had obviously seen the contents of his pocket-book.

'I have a small bag,' Mr Howard admitted, and forestalled my offer to carry it with a swift, 'which I will bring in myself. Do you have a lad to stable my horse?'

'Sarah will see to your horse,' Mother said.

'Sarah seems to see to a great deal,' Mr Howard said, but his smile removed any sting from the words. He stepped outside into the misty darkness and quickly lifted a tarred canvas bag from behind the saddle of his horse. He held it close to him, as if it held some amazing treasure. I am no lover of cold so I huddled deeper into my shawl as I led Mr Howard's brown mare into our miniscule stable and began to remove the saddle and bridle. I could still smell the powder smoke in the air and wondered what had happened out there in the unknown dark beyond the fringe of surf that marked Chale Bay.

Mr Howard had followed me in to the stable and now watched me work, with his head still hatless and his queue pointing neatly downward.

'What is her name?' I asked as I blew into the mare's nostrils and looked deep into her eyes.

'Why do you ask?' Mr Howard was immediately on the defensive.

I looked at Mr Howard as he stood just inside the doorway. He tilted his head slightly to one side and raised his eyebrows. He was handsome enough, I thought, in a rough and tumble sort of manner. Or rather he had been handsome some twenty years or so ago.

'Horses are like people,' I told him. 'They like it better when you call them by name.' I smoothed my hand over the mare's fetlocks, lifted a brush and set to work.

'Her name is Chocolate,' Mr Howard said, and I swear there was nearly a smile in his voice. I liked him better for his choice of name.

"That is a good name," I approved, but I did not lift my eyes to meet his.

Mr Howard was silent for a while but I was aware of his eyes on me as I bent to wash Chocolate's legs.

'I presume you are a local girl?'

"Born and bred in the Island" I told him, as I put the saddle aside and piled the harness on top. It was heavy leather, as battered and scarred by hard usage as its owner but at one time this had been a saddle of the highest quality. I noticed rub-marks on both sides of the crupper where something had hung down, and wondered exactly who Mr Howard was and why he was here. You will forgive my suspicion when you recall that this was1803 and Britain was at war with Bonaparte's France. We on the island were on the front line and fearful of invasion at any time.

'Then perhaps you can help me?' Mr Howard asked. I saw the gleam of silver between his fingers.

'I am not that sort of girl, sir,' I felt my heart begin to thunder; I had heard of men like Adam Howard but had never met one. All the men in the Back of the Wight knew me well enough to let well alone. No man had ever used me ill and I swore I'd give a pretty tannen – that's a hard beating if you do not understand island speak - to the man that tried. I backed toward the pitchfork I always left leaning against an upright in case of a sudden onslaught by the French or a drunken smuggler. I rested my hand on it and tried to look fierce.

'I am not for an instant suggesting anything untoward,' Mr Howard said. He did not look afraid of my scowling face. Instead he gave that small smile again. 'I only require some information that only a local person would know.'

I stopped trying to look as savage as a French guardsman but kept my hand hovering close to the long haft of the pitchfork. 'What sort of information would that be, sir?' I prepared myself to deny any knowledge of the free traders who frequented this part of the Island but Mr Howard surprised me with his request.

'Are you aware of a place called Knighton Hazard?' He held out the silver shilling, keeping it beyond arms-length so I could not quite reach it.

'I am indeed, Mr Howard,' I said. 'It lies slightly inland of here and to the west. It is a large manor house with a dragon weathervane. You can't miss it; there is a folly on a rise beyond the house and a square chapel outside.'

Mr Howard nodded. 'That is what I was told,' he said.

'Then why ask for something you already know?' I asked hotly. 'Are you making game of me?'

'I am not making game of you,' Mr Howard retained hold of his shilling. 'I was merely testing your knowledge.'

Or my honesty, I thought. This Mr Howard had heard of our island way of leading strangers astray.

'Does Mr Bertram still own Knighton Hazard?' Mr Howard asked.

'He still does,' I said, slightly sulkily. I was beginning to not like this handsome man with the battered hat.

'Well and good,' Mr Howard spun the shilling and caught it in the palm of his hand. 'And do you know Limestone Manor?' He finally held out the silver shilling, which I took of course, although I would have imparted with the information for nothing if he had been less offensive. I also knew that Limestone Manor was the real object of his questioning.

'I know it equally well,' I said. I tested the shilling and secreted it inside my boot lest he demand it back. 'It is only a mile or so along the coast.'

'To the east?' Mr Howard's eyes were sharp.

I shook my head. 'To the north west,' I said and pointed in that direction. 'But if you intend to visit sir, you will be wasting a journey. There's nobody there. Limestone Manor has lain empty for years.'

Mr Howard nodded. 'All the same, I think I will take a small ride in that direction tomorrow. Thank you Sarah.' He slipped away from the stable without another word, leaving me to finish stabling his horse and cleaning his equipment. I took my time for I do not care to rush such an important job, besides the poor horse had been ridden hard and needed some attention. Yet all the time I was rubbing Chocolate down I was thinking about Mr Howard. My curiosity forced me to find out more about him, and there was only one way to do that. However, fate had me in its grasp and there was other work for me that night.

Chapter Two

Something had wakened me, although I did not know what. I slipped out of bed and opened the shutters for light. The mist had cleared, maybe chased away by the cannonade, and there was moonlight above the sea. It glinted on the smooth waves that eased northward to hush on the broad sands of Chale Bay and surge up the narrow St Catherine Chine, the narrow gulley- like passage that allowed access from our inn to the shore.

A single strand of moonlight slipped into my room, glinted on the blue pitcher that stood on my table and allowed enough light for me to see by. Do you remember a few short moments ago when I told you that I was curious and intended finding out more about the mysterious Mr Howard? Well that was exactly what I intended to do.

Moving as quietly as a mouse skirting a wakeful cat, I lifted the latch of my door and entered the creaking corridor that connected the rooms in the upper floor of the Inn. I paused here to listen but save for the constant surge and suck of the sea there were no sounds. I stepped out and froze.

'Is that you Sarah?'

Mother had appeared at her door like a ghost, except this spectre was fully dressed in boots and long cloak and carried a couple of canvas sacks over her arm.

'Yes, Mother,' I whispered. I thought quickly. 'I heard a noise.'

Luckily Mother chose to believe my tale. 'That would be me,' she said. 'Throw some clothes on and come outside. Hurry girl, else I will give you a right spat.'

I did not ask further but dressed as quickly as I was able. Mother followed me into my room and watched me to make sure I remembered how to complete the complex procedure of putting on my clothes in the correct order 'Hurry girl,' she repeated, and although I obeyed her as best I was able she gave me the promised spat, which rang bells in my ears. 'Take a bag,' Mother ordered, and threw one across to me. Made from tarred canvas, it was sufficiently deep to hold a whole host of contraband, if that had been Mother's intention.

I was still unsure where we were headed as Mother lifted a lantern from its hook against the taproom wall and we led us out of the inn. The night was clear and cool, with a westerly breeze that carried the hush of the surf to us as we descended the chine to the beach below. Light from Mother's lantern bounced to illuminate our path, as our feet slipped and slithered on the chalk path. I held the hem of my skirt away from the fringe of damp grass, wondering what mother had in mind.

'You'll see, Sarah,' Mother read my mind and told me.

And I did see. We were not alone on the beach. In the flitting light of a cloud-smitten moon, the surf glittered silver along the edge of Chale Bay, with the sea surging deceptively soft as if it had never taken the life of a boat or a sailor-man. Sometimes I hated that sea and at other times I loved it but always I respected it, as Chalkheads do. It was and is part of our lives and even in its most destructive mood it can send bounty to those who live by its edge. There were at least a dozen people walking along the whispering tongues of surf. Occasionally one would bend down and lift something from the water and either crow with delight or throw the object back into the waves.

'There was a ship damaged in that gunfire last night,' Mother explained quickly as if I needed to be told, 'so there will be wreckage washed ashore. We might pick up something useful. The tide is on the flow so anything that got shot away will be coming ashore now.'

I nodded. You may be aware of the meaning of the Horse Head in our inn sign. The horse head is an ancient symbol, granted by the Crown that allows the owner to legally glean flotsam from the beach. Of course all islanders look on whatever the sea gifts us as our right, but in our case it is different. The Bembridges have lived at Chale Bay since God created this Eden, and we have sailed our seas since they were salt, so all that the sea casts us is ours by law and habit for evermore. Amen.

Before I waded into the sea I slipped off my boots for I did not want the salt water to damage them, and neither did I want the labour of cleaning and oiling them later that night. There is enough toil in this vale of tears and joy without creating more. Mother was correct; every surge of the tide carried in more wreckage. There were shattered spars and pieces of shot-ridden timber together with lengths of cable that a group of Ventnor fishermen immediately grabbed and spirited away before somebody challenged their actions.

'There, Sarah: take that!' Mother pointed to a section of fine canvas that gleamed white under her lantern light. 'You can fashion that into some work wear.'

I squeezed off the worst of the water and folded the canvas into my bag. There were other objects: ragged pieces of canvas, a seaman's trousers, a broken chest and unidentified pieces of wood, a few bottles that were most unfortunately empty; all the rubbish that remains from a shattered ship. As you can see, the misfortunes of poor seaman can work to our advantage. We are not wreckers at the Back of Wight, not like the men of Cornwall, yet we do not turn our backs when the sea offers us her bounty. This time, however, the pickings were meagre and as the tide turned the searchers drifted away, some with treasure but most disappointed.

'The ship was damaged,' James Buckett the smuggler said, 'not sunk. There are only bits and pieces to salvage here.'

'And all the better for that,' I said, hotly, glancing at Mother. 'A ship going down means men drowning, wives widowed, daughters and sons orphaned…'

Buckett glowered at me. 'The sea has taken two sons of mine,' he said. 'It owes me.'

I decided to stop being so righteous. 'I'm sorry; I did not know…' I realised that I was speaking to myself as Buckett stalked away.

Mother pointed to a pile of seaweed that floated raggedly on the ebb. 'Have a look there Sarah. I think there's something hidden underneath.'

I did as I was told, pushing aside the sodden tangle and looking beneath. When a man's hand flopped out, all white and limp I recoiled at once. 'Mother!'

Mother was there in seconds, 'is it anything worth having?' She frowned when she saw the hand. 'It's only a dead body, Sarah; dead men don't bite. Check the pockets; there may be money.'

I backed away, shaking my head. 'We can't rob the dead,' I said in genuine shock.

'Oh don't be such a buffle head,' Mother stooped down and pushed aside more of the seaweed. 'How will we give him a proper burial without money? God knows the inn is not making us any just now.' She looked at me and even in the dark of the night I saw the sorrow in her eyes. 'This is somebody's son, Sarah, and maybe somebody's husband. It's not right to deprive him of a Christian burial.'

He had been handsome in life, a tall, brown haired young man with broad shoulders and the whitest skin I had ever seen on a man. When mother pushed away the last of the seaweed I saw he wore nothing at all to cover himself.

'Poor boy,' Mother replaced enough of the seaweed to regain the poor drowned boy his modesty. 'The sea must have ripped his clothes off. It does that sometimes.'

I knew she was thinking of Father and I touched her arm, briefly. Then I thought how this young man must have felt when he was blown off his ship by cannon fire, I could nearly sense the terror in his face. I looked at him, wondering what his last thoughts had been, wondering if he had thought of his mother or his sweetheart, and then I saw a tiny movement in his chest; just a flicker, but enough to catch my interest.

'Mother,' I said, 'he's not dead! Look!' Mother looked and shook her head. 'He's dead as a rat, Sarah. Come on girl, there are no pickings here. We'll attend to the body tomorrow.'

Taking hold of my arm, Mother pulled me away, but for some reason I turned aside, just as the corpse moved again. I shook my arm free. 'Mother; he is alive.'

Despite my mother's tut of disapproval, I knelt beside my naked castaway and placed my ear against his chest. His skin was cold but surprisingly soft beneath the thin coat of crisp dark hair. 'I can hear his heart,' I said. 'Come on Mother.'

Mother may be a bit crousty at times, as we say of women with a touch of temper, but when things need to be done there is nobody better. She whistled as loudly as any carter, and waved to attract the attention of the retreating men. 'We need your hands here now!'

They came of course, half a dozen hang-gallus rascals who were more used to clinging to the yards of a Ryde privateer than in any legitimate employment, but who carried my naked young man up the chine as tenderly as any mother with a new-born babe. Of course, being men as rough as the sea-coast, they worked with muted curses that were followed by quick apologies to Mother. Nobody apologised to me, I noticed, somewhat ruefully. Mother had left the door to the inn open, as was normal in our part of the island, so the men walked in unhindered.

'Up the stairs, lads,' Mother ordered and the carriers clattered and thumped up the wooden stairs, swearing as they inadvertently banged their burden's head against the wall. 'First room on the left; handsomely does it.' I squeezed in front and pulled back the bedclothes. They placed him in the bed, with one scar-faced scoundrel grinning at me as the seaman's nakedness was exposed.

'Don't you be taking advantage of that man now,' he said, and laughed as Mother tutted, gave him a sound slap on the arm and then thanked them all for their kindness with an offer of free ale.

'No need for any of that, Charlotte,' they said, slightly embarrassed.

I did look of course. After all I am as human as you are and some things naturally attract my attention. I would like to say that I was used to a man's nakedness, but that would be a downright lie, which is a sin against God, as the good Reverend Barwis never tires of telling us apparently sinful folk of the parish. In all honesty that was the first full-naked man I had ever seen close to and it was well, not quite what I expected. If anything it was a bit disappointing after the tales of Kitty and the hints of Molly. I had expected more, really.

Mother was watching me, looking sideways with a queer little smile on her face. 'Attend to your work, Sarah,' she said quietly. 'There will be time enough for that sort of thing later.'

I coloured and did as I was bid, albeit with some sly glances that I am sure Mother never noticed. I was sent to fetch warm water and we washed the salt and sand from the unfortunate castaway, removed a few strands of seaweed from his hair and while I prepared a warming pan for his bed, mother slid away the now-wet sheet, replaced it with another and tucked him up as if he was a new-born baby and not a full-grown man.

'There you are, young orphan of the storm,' Mother said quietly. 'You are safe now, whoever you are.' She faced me, level eyed. 'Now you know the rules around here, Sarah; this man has been cast away by the sea and is in our care until he chooses to leave.'

'I know that Mother,' I said.

'And what happens in the Back of Wight stays in the Back of Wight,' Mother reminded, as if I needed to be told.

I glanced across to the door of Mr Howard's room.

'He is away out on some business of his own,' Mother said. 'I don't know what and I don't want to know what.' She hardened her tone slightly. 'And neither do you.'

I nodded. 'I understand, Mother.' In those old days of smugglers and revenue men, of French privateers and marching redcoats, sometimes it was best not to know too much, however inquisitive one's nature happened to be. Mother had warned me not to interfere in Mr Howard's business and not to mention our new non-paying guest to him. That was clear as an April morning.

Chapter Three

The first I knew about the Volunteers was when I woke the next morning to hear the regular tramp of marching feet. Of course I had seen plenty before, for with all the worry about Bonaparte invading, Wight was full of men in scarlet uniforms; regular army, Yeomanry, Volunteers and small boys who had borrowed their father's uniforms and paraded around in danger of a good whipping.

'Sarah!' Mother's roar wakened the whole house. 'Get yourself down here at once and get the shutters off the windows!'

There must have been a hundred of them, stalwart young men in scarlet tunics and white trousers marching toward the inn with their muskets against their shoulders and their feet rising and falling in unison, for all the world like a painted centipede thrumming its way across the ground.

After a blow like the previous evening, of course, the air was fresh and the sky clear, with a stiff breeze kicking white horses off the tops of the waves and the horizon clear as polished crystal as far as my eye could see. There was the usual traffic on the sea; half a dozen coasters, a single Royal Navy cutter searching for free traders in all the wrong places and a couple of three masters braving French privateers and the Press as they pushed eastward for the Downs and the entrance to London. I spent only a moment admiring the view before switching my attention to the marching men.

For all their majesty and pomp, it was not so much the soldiers who attracted my attention, grand though they were, but rather the officers who accompanied them. I was well used to seamen, while despite their increasing presence soldiers were still slightly exotic and therefore interesting. Officers were most fascinating of all, with their glamorous uniforms, gold braid and possibilities of all sorts of wonderful adventures.

The captain in charge was tall, saturnine, handsome and aloof. I watched him ride up and look at our inn as if it was somehow beneath him. Anyway he was at least in his mid-thirties and therefore far too old for me. He was followed by a brace of ensigns, young, fresh faced boys with smart uniforms and eager eyes; I doubt either had turned seventeen yet with their unshaven faces and chubby little cheeks. I was far more interested in the lieutenants. There were two of these, and one walked right into the inn and into my life.

'Good morning,' I greeted him with as wide a smile as I could muster at that time in the morning.

'Good morning to you, too' he replied with a sweeping bow that immediately won me over. When you are used to the grunts and growls of very uncouth mariners, a man of manners is always a rare treat. As the lieutenant straightened up I saw that he was in his early twenties with the most adorable brown eyes and a face that would have put a green sheen of jealousy on any Greek god. 'Are you the proprietor of this delightful inn?' He asked, retaining that wondrous smile.

I could not help my laugh. 'I am afraid not,' I said. 'I am only the daughter of the proprietor. It is my mother you seek, Mrs Charlotte Bembridge.'

The lieutenant bowed again. 'Thank you, Miss Bembridge, although I can see that you are extremely capable of running this establishment with or without the aid of your mother.'

I curtseyed at the compliment, met his eye and could not restrain the blush that accompanied my smile. I lost the latter and retained the former when I heard mother speak and realised that she had been behind me since the lieutenant stepped into the tap room.

'And who are you, sir?' The fact that my mother called him 'sir' at first acquaintance indicated that she had also been captivated by his charm.

'Lieutenant David Baldivere, Ma'am, at your service.' His bow was as low as could be, and more graceful than any Frenchman could manage, I'll be bound. The wonder is that he did not burst his tight breeches. I am sure that my glance in that direction was inadvertent.

'Well, Lieutenant David Baldivere,' Mother said, nearly smiling as he dried her hands on a scrap of clean rag, 'what can I do for you?'

'My men,' the brave lieutenant conveniently forgot the arrogant captain, who remained outside during our conversation, 'are searching for any survivors of a sea battle that occurred last night.'

'Are they indeed?' There was no need for Mother to give me her warning glance. 'I wish you every joy in your search, lieutenant.' The 'sir' had quickly been replaced, I noted.

'Were you aware of the action, Mrs Bembridge? Or you, Miss Bembridge?' When he gave me that wonderful smile I could not help but renew my liking for him. He was only doing his job after all, and not intentionally interfering with our lives.

'That thunder storm last night took all my attention,' Mother spoke for us both.

'Ah,' the lieutenant nodded. 'I understand.' I think he did too, damn his perspicacity. 'You may be interested to know that one of our customs cruisers caught a smuggling lugger making a run from the coast of France to this area.'

'Did they indeed?' Mother looked suitably astonished. 'I hope they captured all the rascals.'

Lieutenant Baldivere shook his head. 'Alas no, Mrs Bembridge. The cutter got off several astute blows and landed a number of shots on the smuggler, but with the stare of the weather and that damn... I do beg your pardon, Ma'am; that dratted mist, the smuggler escaped.'

'Indeed,' Mother frowned, as befitted a patriotic Briton who had no sympathy for free traders who ran silks and spirits from the coast of our enemy directly to our wine cellars. 'Well, better luck next time, perhaps.'

I thought of our naked guest in the room upstairs, only a few yards from this eager and very dashing lieutenant. At least now I knew he was from a smuggling lugger. We would tend him until he was well and then send him on his merry way. I hid my smile; with a bit of luck he may even reward us with a parcel of French silk or even a keg or two of fine French brandy.

'Lieutenant Baldivere,' I said quietly, 'it seems that your men are leaving without you.' I nodded outside the window, where the Volunteers were formed up and beginning to march past with that arrogant captain barking out orders in the most brutal manner. I had conceived as big a dislike for that captain as I had a liking for the lieutenant.

'Oh that matters not,' Lieutenant Baldivere said, 'for I intend to stay at this inn for a day or so, providing that you have a room to spare?'

Now, the Horse Head Inn is only a small place, with two rooms for guests. One was already taken by the mysterious and wealthy Mr Howard, while our unfortunate naked smuggler occupied the other. With groups travelling together, or the rougher sort of travellers, mother would happily double them up in the rooms, but I could not see Mr Howard agreeing to that and it was inconceivable that the lieutenant would share with his prey.

I waited for Mother to inform the lieutenant that there was no room at the inn.

'Of course you can stay, sir,' she said with a broad smile that was as false as a politician's promise, or the propaganda of that ogre Bonaparte. 'Why, you can have Sarah's room, if you don't mind having her female fripperies scattered around.'

About to protest, I held my tongue. Partly because I knew it would do no good, partly because we always needed money and partly because, well, I rather liked the look of Lieutenant David Baldivere and did not really object to his presence in my room. In fact I found the idea strangely appealing in the most disturbing way.

'Oh, no!' The good lieutenant placed a hand on my sleeve, bless him. 'I could not dream of driving this lady out of her room.'

'Oh sir,' I put on all my charm, while hoping that our naked smuggler did not make his appearance now, tumble down the stairs and get us in all sorts of trouble, 'I am quite happy to sleep in the kitchen for such a distinguished guest.' I forbore to mention that I was well used to sleeping in the kitchen for guests who may have been less distinguished but whose coin was equally welcome.

The lieutenant's laugh was genuine. 'I am hardly distinguished,' he said. 'I am the younger son of a parish vicar with no prospects and no talent.'

At that moment I did not care who his parents were or if he had prospects or not. I was much more intrigued with his honesty in telling us about himself right away, and his disquiet about evicting me, a poor innkeeper's daughter, from her bedroom. Such kindness was not usual, in my experience.

'I think you are very distinguished,' I told him, and favoured him with my second best smile. 'And I wager that you have many talents.' I toyed with the idea of allowing my gaze to run down him from his forehead to his feet and back, as Kitty had taught me, but with Mother watching I thought I had better not.

I felt my mother's gaze on me and wondered if she could read my innermost thoughts. As the lieutenant responded to my smile with another of his own,

I could see a golden future stretching in front of me. My vision was a future of glamorous balls at the side of this handsome officer and no more scrubbing floors at the inn, or persuading rough fishermen to go home when they have had too much to drink. I was more than happy at the prospect, although a trifle put out by the thought that poor Mother would have to cope on her own. I stilled my conscience with the knowledge that she could hire a skivvy to do the rough work while she supervised. You may think that my instant leap from first meeting to matrimony was too fast, allow me to remind you that this was wartime, lives were short and cheap and adorable, handsome young men who may accept the hand of an innkeeper's daughter were in short supply.

With Kitty in the vicinity I had to move fast or lose my chance, for Kitty was the most attractive girl with the most shapely body you can ever imagine. After one sight of her men tended to forget that I even existed.

'Now sir, while Sarah takes care of your horse and moves her most personal possessions from your room, may I offer you wine? Or brandy?'

'That is very civil of you, Mrs Bembridge,' my lieutenant said. 'Brandy would be most welcome.'

You notice that there was no qualm about accepting brandy that must be smuggled while searching for the men who had transported that same brandy. It was a case of double standards that always amused me. My handsome Lieutenant Baldivere was no exception and in that he was very much a man of our time.

Chapter Four

'We'll have to get the smuggler out of the house,' Mother whispered to me across the width of the bar counter. 'If this Lieutenant Baldivere catches him here...' She had no need to complete the sentence.

'He's still unconscious,' I said. 'I've just checked.'

Mother swore. Only one word, yet it revealed her state of mind. 'That makes it harder. We'll need help to carry him.' She looked around the tap-room. Business had been quiet these last few weeks, which was one reason why Mother had been keen to allow Lieutenant Baldivere to stay. There were only three people huddled around half-empty pots of ale, with James Buckett and Molly speaking together in low, intense tones.

'James,' Mother said quietly as she approached the smuggling captain. 'Did you hear what happened last night?'

As Buckett looked up the light from the hanging lantern reflected from his gold ear-ring. 'I heard,' he said. 'The revenue say they fired into a free trader.'

'Do you know who she was?' Mother was always direct.

Buckett shook his head. 'I haven't heard anything bar that,' he said. 'Whoever she was, she was not a local craft.' He drained his tankard of ale and screwed up his villainous, salt-pickled face. 'I doubt she was a smuggler at all; more likely some innocent coastal brig. The Excisemen want to look good else they'll all be pressed into the Navy.'

'One of their seamen fell overboard,' Mother lowered her voice.

Buckett's face twisted into a frown. 'Or he was blown over by a revenue cannon-ball.' He looked away. 'Is that the naked fellow that young Sarah rescued?'

'That's the very man,' Mother said.

Buckett lifted his tankard in salute. 'Bully for you, Charlotte, and for Sarah. Is he injurcd?'

'Not badly,' Mother said. 'I had the doctor examine him. He has a bruise on the side of his head where he hit something and a bit of a damaged leg but he should be perfectly all right when he regains consciousness.'

'I will speak to him then,' Buckett said, 'and find out where he is from.'

'There is a problem,' Mother said. 'We have other guests.'

Buckett looked around the tap-room. 'I know these people,' he said, 'they won't blab.'

'I have a lieutenant of Volunteers named Baldivere,' Mother said, 'and a gentleman who gave his name as Adam Howard.'

'Your free-trader can't stay here, then,' Buckett said at once.

'Do you have room for him?' Mother asked.

Buckett shook his head. 'With me and the wife and six little ones the house is stuffed full.'

'I have room,' Molly stopped talking as the door opened and Mr Howard stepped in.

'Ah Mr Howard,' Mother greeted him with an extended hand. 'Welcome back!'

Mr Howard looked around with a slight smile on his face. 'This looks like a very important discussion,' he said.

'There was a sea battle off the coast last night,' I said. 'I was wondering if anybody knew what had happened.'

Mr Howard frowned. 'I had not heard about that.' He sat down, placing his disreputable hat on the table. 'Tell me more, if you will.'

Mother stepped forward. 'I will tell you all I know, Mr Howard. Sarah; go you and attend to Mr Howard's horse. I will see to his lunch.' She pushed me as I hesitated. 'Go on, girl.'

Although I would dearly have liked to stay and listen, I did as I was ordered. I could feel Mr Howard's gaze on me as I left the tap-room and only a few moments later he joined me in the stables.

He sat on a bale of hay and watched as I rubbed down Chocolate's legs.

'She likes you,' he said pleasantly. 'You spend more time caring for her than I do.'

I looked around. 'She is a lovely animal. You can tell a lot about a man by the way his animals act.'

'Is that so?' He sounded sincere. Most men tend to mock the opinions of young women, treating us as if we were simpletons, suitable only for cleaning, cooking and creating babies. Mr Howard seemed different.

'Especially dogs and horses,' I said. 'If a man is nervous, then his dog will be too, and if a man is calm, then his horse will usually be the same. Chocolate has the most lovely nature. She allows me to fondle her without any hesitation. She is a very trusting horse, so she has always been well treated.'

As I spoke, Chocolate lowered her head and nuzzled me.

'She undoubtedly likes you,' Mr Howard said. 'I am glad she is in good hands. Do other people entrust their animals with you? That Captain Buckett for instance; do you care for his horse?'

My guard slammed up straight away. 'I don't believe that Captain Buckett has a horse,' I said.

'Perhaps not,' Mr Howard laughed. 'He is a smuggler I believe.'

'I would not know about that,' I smiled. 'I do know he is a married man.' That was a piece of essentially harmless information designed to disarm Mr Howard.

'I am sure he is,' Mr Howard rose, still smiling. 'You are loyal Sarah; I like that.' He gave a bow that may have been meant in irony and sauntered away, leaving me with Chocolate and my thoughts.

This Mr Howard was as pleasant as be-damned but asked a sight too many questions for my liking. He was a man to watch, yet for all that, I could not help but like him and I felt that my life and his were destined to weave together in some unaccountable fashion.

Chapter Five

My naked smuggler was still unresponsive when we opened his door and slipped in. 'He's not the most handsome looking fellow and no mistake,' Molly whispered as we looked down on him.

'I think he is handsome,' I defended my catch until I saw Molly's face and realised that she was teasing me.

'Oh, you think him handsome, do you?' She said, 'we'd better watch or you will be a-throwing him over your shoulder and running away with him.' She nudged me.

'Rather than ogle, you'd be better employed getting some clothes on him, or people will talk.' Mother and James Buckett had entered behind us, with Mother immediately taking charge. 'Come on Sarah; you can help.'

Have you ever dressed an unconscious man? I can tell you that it is a most interesting procedure that takes a fair bit of labour and quite some manoeuvring to get all the arms and legs in the correct places, not to mention sundry other parts and pieces of the male anatomy. Limbs and things tend to flop around and go into the most awkward shapes imaginable. I tried my best to help, while Mother and James Buckett did the hard work so soon my naked man was no longer naked and, indeed, looked quite the respectable sailor as he lay on top of the bed in breeches, shirt, brass-buckled shoes and a fine blue coat.

'I want that coat back,' Mother said. 'Thomas will be looking for it when he gets home.'

'You'll get it back,' James Buckett said. Nobody mentioned that Father had been missing at sea for some five years now. Only Mother had not given up hope. I knew she would be looking for him coming through the door when she was a wrinkled old woman. That was her way and I thank God for it.

We had worked in hushed whispers for fear of waking Mr Howard, who lay in the adjoining room, and now Buckett carefully opened the door and peered into the landing. It must be the nature of his nocturnal work that he moved quietly, for he made no sound at all as he stepped outside.

Pressing a finger to her lips, Mother inserted a key into the lock of Mr Howard's door and turned it. 'That will keep him out of the way,' she said quietly.

'How about the lobster?' Buckett asked.

'He's out with his regiment, marching up and down to nowhere and looking splendidly scarlet' Mother said. 'We can only hope that he remains outside until we have this fine young fellow safe.'

Nodding, Buckett slipped an arm underneath my castaway's middle, hoisted him across his shoulder and stood up, carrying the man as easily as if he was a sack of wheat, or a keg of fine French brandy. 'Come on, then; lead on Charlotte.'

In truth I was a little sorry to see my not-quite handsome young sailor man carried down the stairs. I had grown used to his company; for all that he was not the best conversationalist in the world. You see, unlike other men in the Back of Wight, he did not cause me any trouble, or seek to pinch me in a certain place or do anything else that was unbecoming to my person or station. I rather liked him in that condition. Maybe there would be less trouble in the world if men were retained in a state of unconsciousness until needed, and then revived with smelling salts for whatever function they were required.

'Sarah!' Mother gave me a vigorous poke in the side. 'Stop daydreaming and get the door open.'

I slipped ahead, nearly falling over my skirt in the process, opened the front door and stopped in shock.

'Hello, Miss Bembridge.' Lieutenant Baldivere stopped in the very act of pushing the door open from the outside. 'Wherever are you going at this time of night?'

I stared, tongue-tied, for it was a situation that I had never envisaged, but luckily Mother was quicker of wit than I.

'Why Lieutenant! I am glad that you have returned,' she said. 'I was wondering if you had been sent overseas at short notice. I was fearful lest you had perhaps posted to the Antipodes, or Scotland or other such ungodlike place.'

Lieutenant Baldivere hastily removed that hat that officers wear and which look so silly perched on their heads. Who on earth devises such a foolish get-up for grown men? I don't know, I really don't.

'I assure you that I am still on Wight,' he said, somewhat unnecessarily as we could see him, plain as the perfect nose on his face. 'Is there some trouble?' He looked concerned as Buckett stopped in front of him with the smuggler draped across his shoulder. 'I say, has that fellow been caught with his fingers in the till?'

I saw Buckett drop a cudgel from his sleeve into his left hand and thought it best to act quickly. It would do Mother's reputation as a host no good at all if a known smuggling master cracked a Volunteer officer over the head at her own front door.

'Why no, sir!' I took the good Lieutenant Baldivere by the arm and hustled him away to allow Mother and Buckett to ease past and into the night. 'This gentleman guest has had a little too much refreshment and Captain Buckett here kindly agreed to help him home.'

Lieutenant Baldivere smiled like the gentleman he was. 'Good Lord! I always heard that the men of Wight were among the most helpful in England. Look here, is there anything I can do to help? I am happy to take a turn at carrying him.'

'Oh there is no need,' Molly joined in the play. 'I'll give him a piece of my mind when I get him home, the drunken sot!' She added weight to her words by landing a full blooded slap on my poor sailor man's person, which was perhaps not the wisest thing to do as he promptly woke up and looked about him.

It must have been a trifle disconcerting for him, for his last memory would be on board a lugger in the Channel, and now he woke up bent across a man's shoulder as a gaggle of women and an officer of Volunteers chatted happily outside a country Inn, but at least my fine young castaway could have had the good sense to remain quiet, or at least speak in English. Oh no, not our silly boy: his first words were in French, which really set the cat among the pigeons and set in trail a whole sequence of events that had me marry my first brace of husbands, as you will see by-and-by.

'*Où suis-je*' he muttered, which I have since been told is: 'Where am I?' in French. It was perhaps not the wisest thing to say in front of a military officer at a time when we were at war with France.

Luckily Lieutenant Baldivere was either hard of hearing or was not the most intelligent of officers. Having got to know him better since then, I would opt for the latter. 'I say,' Lieutenant Baldivere stepped back, 'what did that fellow say?'

It was a situation that called for drastic action, so I took it. Without thinking, I grabbed hold of Lieutenant Baldivere's arms and kissed him, there and then, full on the lips and in front of Mother, Molly and James Buckett. That was also not the wisest course of action in the long run.

'Good Lord,' Lieutenant Baldivere said, when I eventually released him to gasp for breath. And then again he said, 'good Lord.'

Now please don't think that I was in the habit of kissing any stray lieutenant of Volunteers that happened to find me helping carry French-speaking smugglers out of our inn at one o'clock in the morning. That was the first time I had done it, actually, and if truth be told, I have never had the opportunity of doing it since. But at the time it seemed like the best idea and, as he was a personable young man and it was quite a pleasurable act, I did it again, cupping that young officer's face within my hands and pressing my lips against his.

Strangely, he did not seem to object to having a charming inn-keeper's daughter such as I was accost him in such circumstances, and he responded in kind, even having the audacity to put his arms around me and hold me close. I was tempted to slap him for his forwardness but decided that it would be best to wait until Mother, Buckett and Molly had spirited away my young smuggler, if indeed he was a smuggler and not one of these tailed French devils who are all intent on robbery, rape and pillage.

As soon as I realised that the coast was clear, as the local free traders say when there are no Excisemen around to interrupt their landings, I relaxed my grip on Lieutenant Baldivere.

'My dear Sarah,' he was looking at me most oddly, with his mouth agape and his eyes as wide as a night-hunting cat, except with no predatory ideas in his sweet, innocent, stupid head. 'My dear Sarah, I had no idea that you felt like this.'

Well, I did not really feel like this, whatever 'this' may be, but I did know that my heart and pulse were both racing, whether with the excitement at not being discovered or the lack of breath after those two most necessary kisses I do not know. As one thing leads to another, these two kisses led to a third, and then I knew that Molly, Mother and Captain Buckett were far away with that troublesome French-speaking smuggler, or whatever he was.

'Lieutenant Baldivere,' I said, quite breathlessly, 'this is very shameless of us.' I withdrew from his embrace, which was getting a trifle too passionate for my liking, if not for my enjoyment. At that time I was essentially a good girl, you see.

'Oh Miss Bembridge,' Lieutenant Baldivere said at once, colouring up quite prettily. 'I do so beg your pardon. I had no intention of causing you offence or insult.'

Well of course I knew that, as I had instigated the whole procedure, but in such situations it is always better to allow the man to take all the blame. One can wrestle with one's conscience later if one wishes. In my case of course, I had been acting to protect my mother's honour and reputation, as well as the pate of this lieutenant, as Buckett looked quite ready to crack him one with his cudgel.

'Absolutely no offence taken,' I said grandly forgiving my own faults as I savoured the last few moments and wondered if I could steal just one more kiss before packing this very handsome lieutenant up to his room.

'I do confess,' he said, giving a most gracious bow, 'that I am very taken with you.'

'As I am with you, sir,' I conceded, carelessly.

There was that feeling again. That strange prickling sensation and the fleeting vision of a lifetime of regimental balls and glamorous uniforms as my husband's regiment paraded all along the south coast preparing to meet a French invasion. You will notice that there was no thought of life after the war. This was in 1803, the war had started in 1793 when I was ten years old and save for a short period of armed truce, had continued ever since. We really could not conceive of a time when there might be peace, or when any strange sail off the coast might not be a French privateer or the harbinger of an invasion fleet.

'I do believe,' Lieutenant Baldivere said, and stopped. 'I believe,' he said again, and then: 'Pray excuse me, Miss Bembridge.' Without waiting for my permission he dashed up the stairs to my bedroom and closed the door. I never did hear what he did believe for only then did I hear poor Mr Howard trying to escape from his room, so I hurriedly unlocked his door and prepared to face a barrage of accusations.

Instead he thanked me politely. 'It appeared that the key must have turned in the lock during the night,' Mr Howard said.

'Indeed so, sir,' I agreed with my face as expressionless as a priest caught with a lady of the night. 'These things happen sometimes.'

'Yes.' Mr Howard carried a candle in a brass candle-holder and wore a most fetching night shirt on which somebody had spent many hours embroidering a very neat row of anchors and lions. 'I thought I heard voices.'

'Indeed, sir,' I said. 'One of the guests was three sheets to the wind and had to be escorted home, while Lieutenant Baldivere has only now returned from duty with the Volunteers.'

'That will be it, then,' Mr Howard accepted my excuses readily. 'And you are here to deal with both situations.'

'Indeed sir,' I said. 'Mother and others of our customers were also present.'

'You really are a most capable young woman,' Mr Howard ran his gaze up and down me, as if I were some specimen of animal to be examined, or a bag of potatoes perhaps.

'Thank you sir,' I bobbed in a curtsey even as I wished that this intelligent, questioning man would return to bed where he belonged. Why are some men so inquisitive? The world is all the better for fewer questions and more under-standing and a woman such as me had a job to do.

'I will bid you good night, sir,' I gave out a strong hint, which thankfully he took.

'Good night, Sarah.' His brows closed in a furrow. 'Where do you sleep, Sarah?'

'Why in the kitchen sir,' I said, and added, 'with a cutlass at my side in case of intruders.' Or in case some handsome man of about forty should think I am there for his pleasure, I thought to myself.

'Good night then,' Mr Howard said, and closed his door. I noticed that he retained his key, damn his suspicious mind.

Now you must agree that bluebells are amongst the prettiest of nature's flow-ers as they spread around the ground and in the small copse and woods that decorate the Back of Wight. In my opinion, the bluebells that enhance Long Stone, a few miles west of the Horse Head Inn are the loveliest in the island and that is where I chose to lead Lieutenant Baldivere. It was a beautiful morn-ing in early May, a lone cuckoo was calling and a mating pair of oystercatchers graced the sky above.

I had not had long to wait before Lieutenant Baldivere was free of his Vol-unteer duties; indeed these duties did not seem overly onerous even on a busy day, so I held out my hand to grasp his and drew him up to the grassy downs that stretch far along the south coast of my island.

'To where are you taking me?' Lieutenant Baldivere asked.

'You'll see,' I told him, for I knew the name would mean nothing to an Overner.

'Is it far?'

'Only a few miles,' I said.

'Then we shall ride,' said my handsome lieutenant.

And ride we did. Lieutenant Baldivere had his own mount, a pretty piebald named Prince, while I borrowed Kitty's filly Alexandria, named after the battle in which brave General Abercrombie trounced the French. I was sure that Kitty would not mind so I neglected to inform her. We were after all the most amiable of companions.

I shall never forget that ride, or the few perfect hours that followed it. We were young and, save for the fear of French invasion, carefree, with all our lives in front of us, the wind in our hair, warm horseflesh between our legs and the pounding of hooves as thrilling as always when we trotted across the downs. We passed from St Catherine's Down to Chillerton Down, and on to Limerstone and Brighstone Down. There is a fine manor house at Mottistone but we ignored that as I led my captive to the Long Stone, a place which you will hear a great deal about if you continue with my story, for it is a romantic place and I am a wildly romantic person.

'That is amazingly impressive,' Lieutenant Baldivere said and I liked him all the more for his appreciation of my favourite spot in all of Wight.

You may know the Long Stone for it is famous the length and breadth of the island, and with reason. In the very old days the druids or some such pagan peoples raised great lumps of stone to worship the moon or the sun or the stars or other pagan god, much as the French in their ignorance worshipped Bonaparte. Well, Wight has two such stones, one lying recumbent on the ground and the other standing upright nearby as a testimony to the ignorance of our forefathers. Yet for all its pointlessness, it is a focal point in the landscape and, more important, many young lovers took their sweethearts here for whatever reason. I have been fascinated by this unsightly chunk of stone since my childhood and still am, as you may see presently.

So it was that when we dismounted at the Long Stone with the bluebells spreading prettily all around us, I already had Lieutenant Baldivere in the palm of my hand.

'This is indeed a heavenly spot,' the lieutenant enthused as we stood in the shadow of that great lump of stone and admired the view of the downland and the chopped waves of the Channel. Or rather he admired the view of the downland and I admired the closer view of my own officer of Volunteers.

'It is one of my favourites,' I said, which was a complete truth as I had the habit of visiting this sacred place whenever I needed space to think. However, sometimes a truth can be useful as a means to an end and I had a very specific end in view, as you should be aware by now. 'What is your favourite view?' I asked innocently.

Now any sensible man, standing beside a young woman as charming and personable as I knew myself to be, should take the hint and at least mention her in his next sentence. My Lieutenant Baldivere was obviously not schooled in the correct methods of etiquette according to that great teacher, Kitty Chillerton, so instead he said:

'I do like the view from Westminster Bridge in London.'

'Oh,' I said, realising that he needed some gentle guidance as to the correct response. 'And is there anything you see here that takes your fancy?'

He looked around, 'I do like the sweep of the coast' he said, so I stepped in front of him and waved my arms. 'Oh,' he said as some sort of realisation seeped into his brain. 'I do like to see you, of course.'

'I am glad you said that,' I told him, wondering whether I should slap his face or just leave him there, mount Alexandria and return to the Horse Head. I decided to give him another chance, which was very generous of me, you will allow.

We smiled to each other as we stood beside that great lump of stone. Stretching my arms, I put them behind his neck, pulled him closer and kissed him yet again. I was wondering how often I had to kiss that man before he took the hint, but perhaps there was something magical about the Long Stone for it was not long before he responded with a will and his tongue played the snake-dance with mine .

'Now that was better,' I said when we parted.

He did not say much in return, but his eyes were hotter than I had ever seen them as he for once took the initiative and pulled me in an embrace that was a little clumsy at first but soon relaxed into something much less seemly and far more desirable for us both.

'I do believe that I am falling in love with you,' my handsome lieutenant of Volunteers told me when we broke our embrace once more.

'I do believe that the feeling is mutual,' I replied.

'Oh,' the lieutenant looked at me with his eyes bright with new-found confidence. 'I know,' he said, 'I think we should go the full course and get married.'

I kissed him again, wordless.

That kiss lasted longer than the previous ones and when we parted both Lieutenant Baldivere and I realised that we had made some sort of commitment to each other. We held hands for a while, quietly smiling, and kissed once more. I am not sure if I was frustrated or relieved. After hearing all Kitty's stories I expected something far more dramatic but it was not to be with that very handsome young officer.

Now that the informalities were dispensed with, we remounted our respective horses and returned to the Horse Head, riding side by side and nearly, but not quite, knee to knee across the Downs. I was in a bit of a dream of course, with my future so neatly and quickly decided, for until Lieutenant Baldivere entered my life I had not really contemplated any man as marriage material. With no dowry or any such thing, I had nothing to offer any man of substance, and I certainly was not inclined to throw my life away to a fisherman or a foremast sailor. Oh, I know that many of them were worthy men in their own right, honest as the Gospels and as hard working as the labours of Samson – or was it Hercules? - some big strong man anyway, but fishermen had a habit of getting themselves drowned and seamen were forever going on long voyages that lasted for years, or being pressed into the navy and getting killed. I saw my brave Volunteer lieutenant as much better marriage material; after all, the Volunteers merely paraded around the country looking glamorous. Nobody ever heard of any of them actually becoming involved in the shooting and killing part of war, did they?

Did they?

So I was all a-flutter with excitement when Lieutenant Baldivere approached Mother that evening in the tap-room, and in front of everyone, if you please, asked for a private audience. He had no decorum that man; none at all.

Chapter Six

'Mrs Bembridge,' my handsome lieutenant said, 'may I speak to you, please?'

Mother looked at him with some suspicion, probably wondering if he was going to say that he could not pay his account, or ask for extra fresh linen or some such. 'You are speaking now,' she told him, in rather more severe a tone than she normally used with her guests.

'It is rather a delicate matter,' he said, looking to me for support, or perhaps checking that I had not decided to kiss a farmer next, or one of the hairy free traders.

Mother also glanced over to me, her eyes narrowed. I could nearly hear her thoughts as she wondered what we had been up to and if she would soon have to endure unwanted grandchildren infesting her neat and clean inn. 'Speak,' she said in a voice that would have scared Boney's Old Guard back to Paris.

'I know I should talk to Miss Bembridge's father, Mrs Bembridge, but as he is not here I will ask your permission to marry your daughter.'

Mother's eyebrows rose higher than I had ever seen them rise before. 'You have only known each other a couple of days,' she pointed out. 'Surely a little caution will be in order here?'

'We love each other,' Lieutenant Baldivere said.

'Do you?' Mother's look at me could have penetrated the hull of a man-o-war.

I nodded, thinking of balls and gowns and escape from scrubbing floors.

'Have you?' Only two words, but they asked everything that mattered.

We said nothing. Lieutenant Baldivere and I looked at each other and then at Mother.

'We have not done anything untoward,' I said.

'I would do nothing to impugn the honour of Miss Bembridge,' Lieutenant Baldivere said. 'Indeed I would not.'

'You have not known each other's bodies,' Mother was as direct as ever. I looked around the tap-room, aware that whatever was overheard in here would be the talk of the Back of Wight before the next day dawned. Honestly, Boney was said to have an extensive intelligence service to gather information right across Europe. There was no need: all he needed do was whisper a secret in the Horse Head and half the world would know, especially if Kitty Chillerton was of the company. Conversely, if he desired to know anything, he need only ask Kitty and she would tell him.

'We have not.' Lieutenant Baldivere drew himself as erect as if he was on the parade ground. 'I swear on oath that we have not.'

'Then why the devil must you rush into marriage?' Mother shook her head and allowed that question to float, unanswered, around the room. 'And, Lieutenant, I hear enough oaths in here every night without hearing any more from you.' She looked at me. 'And you can stop looking so righteous and holy, madam. You know as well as I that there are no secrets in Wight so we may as well say all that has to be said now rather than let it leak out in dribs, drabs and rumours.'

'We are not rushing,' I said, grabbing hold of my lieutenant's hand as my vision of a lifetime of ceremonial balls as an officer's wife returned. 'We love each other.'

Mother nodded slowly. 'Then I have no objections. Work out the details between you and let me know. Now, Miss Bembridge, you have work to do.' She looked up. 'Oh; congratulations to you both. Now, Sarah, go and serve poor Mr Howard, he has been waiting at his table for the past five minutes.'

So that was that, all neatly decided and approved. Husband number one was lined up, primed, permissioned, prepared and ready for the altar.

Chapter Seven

'So you are to marry a lieutenant of Volunteers?' Kitty was nearly dancing with excitement as she accompanied me to Molly's cottage deep in the rolling downs.

'I am. I will be Mrs Lieutenant David Baldivere.' I repeated the name, rolling the syllables around my mouth as I savoured the idea. 'Mrs Baldivere; how wildly delicious.'

'So you have had a mysterious guest in the inn, a naked man washed up on the beach and got yourself engaged to an officer all in a few days,' Kitty grabbed hold of my arm. 'Oh tell me all, tell me all, Sarah dear.'

So I did, without embellishments or exaggerations. Or rather without many embellishments or exaggerations for with Kitty one must always add little bits here and there to titillate the Kittylate. She responded well, with many an 'oh' and an 'ah' of appreciation as we strode over the downs to Molly's cottage and many a grabbing-of-my-arm at the juicer bits and many a question that concerned anatomical details that I will not sully this page by printing. I'd probably just create ink- blots anyway, in my excitement.

'Is it true that he is French? I heard that your naked sailor was a Frenchman?'

I should have realised that even such a secret as that would slip out on Wight.

'It is true,' I said solemnly. I also know that even such a terrible thing would pass around all the Caulkheads without ever seeping through to a single Overner. We have a way of keeping things to ourselves that has been developed well through our history of smuggling and such like. After all, we were an independent kingdom once, and one of the last places in England to drop paganism and embrace Christianity.

'Is it true?' Kitty stopped me in the middle of a field, holding my sleeve as if her life depended on it. Her eyes were as wide as the midsummer sun. 'Is it true that Frenchmen have tails?'

I should have expected that question. In England, we believed that the French had tails you see, among so many other strange things. Why, I heard that when a monkey was cast ashore higher up the Overner coast, the local people hanged it in the belief that it was a Frenchman, such was their ignorance.

'It is not true,' I told her solemnly.

'Are you sure?' Kitty was not to be gainsaid. 'Did you check?'

'I did check,' I said. Now that was a downright lie. I had not checked for a tail although as far as I could see all his other anatomical details were exactly the same as any Englishman.

'Oh,' Kitty sounded disappointed. I rather believe she had hoped for a tailed and horned devil washed up by the sea. 'If he has not woken yet,' she said, 'then I shall check for myself. If he has no tail then he cannot be French and there must be some mistake.'

With Kitty being the stubborn puss she is, I could in no way shake her from her decision.

I must describe Molly's home before we proceed, so bear with me for a few moments as I deviate from my story slightly. The geography and setting of Wight has to be understood you see, or you will be lost wandering around our gentle slopes and tiny, meandering roads that can lead to places that have been hidden for generations so only the locals know about them. Molly's cottage was one such, a small, crooked, quaint sort of house with a thatched roof that sagged in the middle and a garden filled with all sorts of flowers and the most amazing selection of herbs that you could ever conceive. It sat in a small dip, with a fringe of trees as shelter from the wind and any casual passers-by, with a pall of blue smoke hazing the building and Molly's own animals lowing and baa-ing in her own small fields all around.

Unusually for the Back of Wight, Molly kept goats, aye, and milked them too, so these uncanny creatures with their devilish green eyes watched us as we slithered across the short grass of the slope. The windows of the cottage also watched for they were eyes as they peered out from under their raggle-fringe of thatch, small, four-paned windows on ground and upper floors all reflecting the sun. The green painted door of course was the nose and mouth of the cottage which had a face and character unique to itself.

I have mentioned elsewhere that Molly was a bit of a witch, so that many people were a-feared to come close to her, which was one reason Mother was so keen to unburden ourselves of our tame Frenchman on her. We know that the authorities, either the Excisemen or the Volunteers would be searching for him, so where better a place to hide him than a house where nobody looked?

Even Kitty, a Caulkhead in her bones and blood, was ever so slightly apprehensive about coming to such a place and she shied away from the goats as if they would eat her, which was possible as they seemed to eat everything else they came across, even, on one occasion, chewing at Mother's straw hat. Oh, she gave them such a spat that time that they never came near her again!

'Come along Kitty, dear,' I said, dragging her past the goats. I scratched the nearest between its horns and it butted me in a friendly fashion. Rather like a young lieutenant of my acquaintance, I thought, except for the green eyes.

'About time you came to see your young man,' Molly said as we came to her door. 'In you come, ladies.'

Kitty rushed in first, safe from the savage goats.

The interior of Molly's cottage was as crooked and uncanny as the exterior, with small rooms of irregular shapes, furniture I am sure survived since the Jutes first colonised the island and beams hung with plants and herbs and only God knew what else. Of course there was a black cat a-sitting by the fire, purring as it scrutinised us through yellow eyes as inscrutable as the goats outside.

'I've put your sailor-man upstairs,' Molly said, as both Kitty and I made a line for the cat. His name was Merlin and he was quick to purr at the attention. 'He's wakened once or twice and slipped back again.'

We were anxious to see our poor captive Frenchman and I lifted Merlin and ran up Molly's wooden steps. I knew the stairs had been carried inland from the wreck of a Dutch galliot some hundred or so years ago and not fashioned locally yet they fitted perfectly into the cottage. That is to say that they were out-of-place, out-of-time and perfectly eccentric.

My Frenchman lay still, much as he had been in the Horse Head, with his face looking a trifle ragged under his young beard. I looked at him, aware of the strangest of sensations that I could not put words to describe. I suppose proprietorial would be the best I could do, as if I owned this orphan of the storm. Which was patent nonsense of course; he was merely a castaway mariner and a foreigner and enemy to boot. Yet I smiled as I looked down upon him, allowed

Merlin to run free back to his cosy seat downstairs and touched the incipient beard of my Frenchman with my forefinger. It was jagged.

'He's a handsome rogue isn't he?' Molly was behind us, although I don't know how we all fitted into that tiny room without dying of claustrophobia. It must have been some more of Molly's magic tricks, making the room stretch to accommodate us all.

I agreed of course, while Kitty, more demanding, screwed up her face in disdain. 'I suppose some may call him that' she said. 'He is sort of handsome, for a Frenchman!'

He certainly was not as classically handsome as my own Lieutenant. Nobody was, yet in his own way, with his monkey-face and broad chin he could be regarded as interesting; for a Frenchman, as Kittie said. Sometimes that woman had the most amazing perspicacity. At other times, she was so wide of the mark she was using a crooked bow and corkscrew arrows.

'Has he wakened at all?' I asked.

Molly nodded. 'Only for a very brief spell,' she said. 'He woke, gabbled a lot of foreign gibberish and dropped away again.'

'He might be one of Boney's spies,' Kitty said, 'come to see what he have in the island worth robbing and ravaging.' I could see her eyeing my Frenchman up, no doubt wondering if he was about to leap out of bed to start the ravaging process, and wondering what position she should put herself into to best accommodate him.

'Not much use in spying with his eyes fast shut,' Molly said. 'It's more likely he's from some privateer or maybe even a Brittany fishing boat.'

My heart sunk at Molly's words. I had no desire to think of my monkey-faced Frenchman as something as mundane as a fisherman. We had plenty of fishermen from Shanklin and Ryde and they were decent men but pretty ordinary. I wanted my pet Frenchman to be a privateersman at least.

'I will leave you to look at your prize,' Molly said. 'I have my animals to attend to.' She looked at me. 'You may wish to shave him soon. There's a razor in the drawer at the side.'

'Shave him?' I said, alarmed at the thought of me let loose with an open razor on the face of this unsuspecting sailor. I realised that Molly had already vanished; she had the knack of disappearing without a sound. That was another reason why people thought her a witch.

'I must see for myself,' Kitty spoke in a low whisper. 'I must check.'

'You must check what?'

'If he has a tail,' that foolish woman said.

'Of course he has not!' I said hotly, although there was just the tiniest bit of me still harboured a doubt. After all, I had not been specifically checking that part of him and perhaps there had been just a vestige of a tail there. 'It is not right to look at the poor foreign fellow when he is all unconscious.'

'That's the beauty of it, Sarah,' this amazing woman said. 'He won't know! We will have a little peek to satisfy our curiosity and that will be the end of it.'

'I don't have any curiosity,' I began, and then I pondered for a moment. Of course Kitty was right. It was educational, for we had long thought that Frenchmen had tails, and he would never know. Perhaps there was the slightest suspicion of another, more basic reason which I will never admit to, but Kitty was most insistent, Molly was away on some animal-related work of her own, the sun was sending friendly beams of dust-mote laden light onto the bed and my Frenchman looked so accommodating and handsome in his ugly, foreign way.

Sighing to signify that I did not approve, yet with more than a trace of excitement, I helped Kitty fold back the covers. My Frenchmen had been stripped to his borrowed linen shirt and lay there on his back, eyes closed and his chest rising and falling gently and rhythmically. As I watched him I once again experienced that feeling of ownership, which Kitty spoiled by taking hold of his nightshirt around his thighs and carefully rolling it back.

'No,' I hissed urgently. 'This is not right! Leave the poor fellow some dignity.'

'I'm just having a look,' Kitty sounded most disappointed. And so she should, the conniving minx.

'Not at that part.' I stood between her and her victim, determined that my Frenchman should be shown at least a modicum of respect.

Kitty's glower and deep sigh were both meant to shame me. Instead I stood my ground. 'We'll roll him over,' I said, 'and have a quick look and then tuck him back up.'

Eventually Kitty agreed. She knew she had no choice, for once my mind was made up; nothing on God's earth would change it. I was more obstinate than the most stubborn of mules. In fact I was even more inflexible than Kitty, or a whole litter of Kitties.

Placing our hands under him, we rolled the poor unsuspecting Frenchman onto his face. He gave an involuntary grunt as we did this and then he was face down on the bed with his shirt a-tangle around his legs and his face all squashed against the pillow. Not that Kitty cared about his poor face at that moment.

'I'll do it,' I said as I gently took hold of the man's shirt, allowing my hand to brush against his curved parts as I did so.

'No; let me,' Kitty nearly pushed me aside in her eagerness to search for a tail. I was surprised how tender she was as she lifted my Frenchman's nightshirt and eased it upward to reveal slender but well-shaped and muscular thighs and a pert bottom that I could not help but admire anew.

'See,' I hissed, 'he's made just as we are. Not a sign of a tail.'

'I'm sure he has one,' Kitty bent closer and began to probe at the appropriate place with her fingers.

'Enough of that, you shameless baggage!' I pulled her away quite violently, so she overbalanced and nearly fell in that crowded room. Reaching out for support, Kitty grabbed hold of the first thing she could, which just happened to be the Frenchman's leg. Her nails scraped down his calf, wakening him and so he opened his mouth and yelled in justifiable surprise. The noise alarmed Kitty, who screamed in sympathy as she slid to the floor, dragging the poor Frenchman's leg down with her; I joined the vocal chorus and all three of us were screeching and yelling like Vectis banshees.

'What's wrong? What's all the noise?' Molly was at the door, looking as alarmed a woman can be when she finds her two female guests all a-tangle with a near naked man on the floor of her upstairs bedroom. As soon as she saw us she began to laugh, and no wonder. Kitty was spread-eagled on her back and the Frenchman on top with his shirt around his waist, his legs and rump all bare to view and me looking and yelling and not quite sure what had happened.

'Up you get,' Molly lifted the Frenchman to his feet with a single hoist and helped him gently back into the bed. 'So you're awake are you?'

The Frenchman looked at her, dazed, and said something incomprehensible in French.

'Can you speak English?' I knelt at the bedside quite ignoring Kitty, who continued to lie on the floor, although her screaming had stopped, thank the Lord.

My Frenchman looked up at me, his eyes blank and the most wondrous shade of green. 'Are you an angel?' He asked, quite distinctly in English. 'Am I in heaven?'

'You do speak English!' I said, 'and with the sweetest accent imaginable.'

He smiled a trifle uncertainly. 'It is the accent we all have where I come from,' he said. 'Are you an angel?'

'I am not an angel. I am only a girl.'

'Oh,' he said. 'That is good. You look like an angel to me,' and with those words my Frenchman promptly slipped away into unconsciousness once more.

'Oh, you…' I felt like slapping him, I really did, but one does not do such things to shipwrecked French sailors, especially when they have such an interesting physiography – if that is the correct word to describe his face, features and all other factors of his build and appearance. Instead I shook my head and stepped back.

'Your mother will be expecting you at the inn,' Molly said. 'You can't stay here ogling stray French sailors all day.'

'Did you hear that Sarah is to be married?' Now that my tail-less Frenchman with the attractive accent was once more in a state of swoon and all covered up, Kitty lost interest in him and turned her attention to me.

'I heard that,' Molly said. 'You are to be congratulated, Sarah. Lieutenant Baldivere seems a most respectable gentleman, although without any funds to speak of.'

I smiled. I had nearly forgotten about the good lieutenant in all the excitement about meeting my Frenchman. Now that I remembered, my heart was all a-flutter with renewed expectation of my exciting life to come. Suddenly I could hardly wait to be back with him. This Frenchman with his penchant for falling asleep would be perfectly safe with Molly, unless Kitty chose to peruse any more of him of course. I could not allow that.

'Come, Kitty,' I said, quite severely, 'It is time that I returned to the inn and I shall not leave you to walk home alone with the island over-run with stray Frenchmen and gurt grockles such as Mr Howard.' A gurt grockle, in case you are not from our island, is a great stranger, and Mr Howard was certainly that. I had not forgotten that particular gentleman and his incessant questioning, for all the visitations of Frenchmen and handsome Volunteers. I grabbed hold of Kitty's arm and hustled her out of the house.

Chapter Eight

'You cannot continue to call me Lieutenant Baldivere,' my handsome officer said with a smile. 'My Christian name is David; you must call me that now.'

I curtseyed my thanks, determined that all should be well between us and a trifle apprehensive lest my lieutenant be scared off once he realised that I was only an inn-keeper's daughter and he was an officer who held the king's commission.

'David it is,' I said. 'Thank you, sir.'

'Come, Sarah,' he put emphasis on my name as if to show me that he wished us to be on such familiar terms, 'we are to be man and wife. We should not have to thank each other for such inconsiderable trifles as using our given names.'

I curtseyed again. We stood outside the Horse Head with a cold wind lifting the tops off the waves in Chale Bay and a company of David's Volunteers lounging around, doing anything except look military as they chewed tobacco or gossiped or even quaffed Mother's ale at prices she had just increased for their benefit. Some just sat on the coarse grass or leaned against the wall of our garden and glowered at the officers.

'What are your men doing?' I asked.

'We are just back from a search of the island,' David told me seriously. 'Captain Chadwick is certain that there is a smuggler hiding somewhere among the fields and thickets so we have spent the day scoring the fields.'

'Did you have any luck?' I asked, sweetly innocent.

'None,' David dropped his voice. 'Between you and I, dear Sarah, I doubt that there is any smuggler at all. All we are doing is giving the men healthy exercise, which is good for them. They do worship their officers, you see, and need to be kept busy lest they get bored.'

I nodded. The Volunteers looked as happy as Job in the midst of his trials or the French nobility when told that the guillotine was oiled and ready to be used. Truly I have never seen a more jaded and ill-tempered bunch of men.

Mother pulled me aside. 'This lot have hardly a farthing to scratch themselves with. They will be on their way soon and not a blade of grass will miss their company.'

I nodded. 'I don't care much for the private soldiers,' I said, 'they look as if one smile would crack their faces.'

'Not surprising that they are unsmiling,' Mother said. 'Most of them no more volunteered than the seamen in the Navy. Their landlords ordered them to don the King's uniform or their family would be evicted, so it was Hobson's choice for them.' She nodded toward David. 'Now go and spend some time with your man. Unless you need a chaperone?'

'No, thank you, Mother,' I said quickly, and nearly ran across to David, who was in the act of dismissing his sourpuss men.

I watched as he called them all to attention, so the unhappy mob turned into three scarlet lines of men all neatly facing their front, with expressionless faces and the heavy Brown Bess muskets held close to their bodies.

'All right men,' David said as he walked the length of the front line, adjusting a piece of equipment here and straightening a shako there, much like a mother checking her children before sending them to church on a Sunday. 'We did not find that smuggler today but it was a valuable exercise for when we hunt Boney back to Paris!'

If David expected a cheer for that he was deeply disappointed, for the only response was sullen silence.

'Now dismiss; get back to your wives and families and we will continue our search tomorrow.'

The men moved away, some erect, others round-shouldered and many grumbling. I compared that lot to my monkey-faced Frenchman and wondered how the Volunteers would fare if ten thousand French soldiers, veterans of Bonaparte's Northern Italian and Egyptian campaigns landed on Wight and marched inland. The thought was a bit too sobering for me to linger over so I concentrated on David instead.

'When shall we name the day?' I asked.

'Very soon I hope,' David said. 'For only this morning we were informed that the regiment is being posted to Dublin.'

'Dublin?' I had only been off the island three times in my life; David travelling as far away as Dublin was something I had never considered. 'How romantic!' I thought for a moment. 'But is Dublin not in Ireland?'

'It is the capital of Ireland,' David extended my education. 'It is one of the most handsome and romantic cities anywhere, with fine architecture and beautiful parks.'

'Oh,' I said, thinking of something to say that did not sound too silly. 'I will miss you when you are in Dublin.'

'Officers may take their wives,' David said softly. 'We are marching in two months.' He put a strong hand on my shoulder. 'We need to get the banns read soon, and decide in which church we will get married.'

I smiled at that. 'Why, David,' I said, 'I know the exact place.'

Chapter Nine

'This is Knighton Hazard,' I stopped outside the eighteenth century mansion with the great sweeping stairs that led to the front door and the worn stone pediment above. 'Sometimes we call it the dragon house because of the dragon weather-vane,' I pointed upward in case David did not know where we Wight people habitually place weather-vanes.

'That is a good name,' David said, 'and this is a fine establishment. Who owns it?'

'Mr Hugo Bertram,' I said. 'He is an interesting man who has tried to encourage couples to marry in his private chapel. I don't know if anybody had ever agreed, though.'

'Oh, I see; how kind of him,' David's habitual smile broadened. 'What an amiable fellow.'

'Mr Bertram got married in there, as did his father and grandfather,' I said, cleverly taking David's hand as I led him through the grounds. There were three other buildings beside the mansion itself. There was the stable block, around ten times larger than the average cottage; there was a folly sitting on a rise so it dominated the landscape, and there was the chapel with a classical exterior that matched the house, plus a spire topped by a Celtic cross and a small, squat tower. Trust the Bertrams to go the whole hog and have one of everything.

'Is it open?' David asked as we stood outside the chapel with its high, arched windows with their stained glass designs.

'Mr Bertram always keeps the doors open,' I said. 'He says that the good Lord never locks anybody outside so why should he.'

David nodded. 'He must truly be one of the most amiable fellows alive.'

I looked around. Further to the west and closer to the coast I could see the tall trees that masked Limestone Manor, with which Mr Howard had seemed so interested. I vowed that I would find out what his fascination was, one of these days; unless David took me away before then, of course. The grounds of Limestone ran adjacent to those of Knighton Hazard, but while Mr Bertram had his lands groomed to perfection and tilled and planted to the utmost, those of Limestone were unkempt and neglected. Every piece of land needs an owner, you see, especially in times of national danger. Every man needs a woman to own him too, of course, lest he goes off the straight and narrow and starts to drink and gamble. I would make sure that David did neither of these things. Or not too often anyway.

Still holding hands, we stepped inside the chapel. It was not the first time I had been inside yet I had never properly looked around me, so please permit me to describe the interior of this place that I came to know uncommonly well.

The chapel was a perfect cube, with a large square headed door as a main entrance and a smaller door at the side that presumably led to a private domain for the vicar. There were two round-headed stained glass windows on each of the three walls that did not contain the entry door, and a portrait flanking each side of that same door.

Rows of pews faced a stone altar that was decorated with the most unusual carvings.

'Roman,' David recognised at once as he stalked toward it, dragging me behind him and so enthusiastic that I am sure he forgot that I was attached to his hand. I staggered and grabbed the altar for support.

'What do you think?' I said, recovering from my stumble and attempting to extricate my hand from his grasp. Once I succeeded I counted my fingers, ensuring that David could see me so he did not act in such a cavalier manner again. He was excellent raw material but needed a lot of training before he was a fit husband.

David looked around the chapel. 'It is beautiful,' he said. He focussed on the two portraits that flanked the main entrance. 'Who are these two?'

'Those are Mr and Mrs Ebenezer Bertram,' I said. 'The chapel and house were built for them.' The portraits caught their likeness exactly, with Mr Ebenezer Bertram in the brilliant scarlet of his full hunting fig, sitting proud on his horse with his dogs at heel and a gaggle of his male children watching from a respectable distance. Across the other side of the door, Mrs Bertram was splendid in a ball gown of shimmering silk, with her hair tall in the fashion of the period and a fan in her hand. Children of the female variety surrounded her in a watchful knot.

'Very amiable,' David said. Giving me an equally amiable peck on the cheek, he once more gripped my hand and closed the door. 'Now we are alone,' he said.

'We are,' I agreed. 'Can you imagine getting married in here with all your officer friends in their gorgeous uniforms on one side of the chapel and all the people from the Back of Wight on the other?' I looked around. 'It will indeed be a most splendid occasion.'

I could nearly hear the vicar giving his sermon and the ripple of comments from the congregation. Oh, I could imagine poor Kitty's face, bright green with envy as she realised that I had beaten her to the altar and she was to be left on the shelf, an old maid compared to my new status as a married woman, and to an officer of good family.

'It will be the most fun,' David said, which I thought a strange way of talking, until his arm snaked around my waist and he pulled me closer to him than I then had a mind to go.

'David,' I laughed, thinking it a jape, 'pray release me. This is not the place and there will be time for that after we are man and wife.' I was still very naïve you see, and believed in the honour of his birth and commission.

'This is a very fine place and time,' he said, with his breathing suddenly ragged and his arm tightening.

'Let go of me!' I demanded. 'Let me be!' I tried to slap at him with my left hand; my right being pinioned by his arm, you understand.

He bowed to me, stopping my protests with his mouth as he kissed me. In other circumstances that would have been a very welcome kiss, but at that moment I did not like David very much, much as I thought I loved him.

'David!' I pulled my mouth away, 'stop that at once!'

'I thought you loved me,' he said. 'We are to be married in here!' His left hand slipped behind me and onto my rump, grabbing hold in a manner a little too rough for my liking.

'David!' I screamed, and then there was another voice and another person in the chapel.

'Enough of that, my bucko!' I recognised James Buckett's harsh voice as David's hands suddenly relaxed and I broke free, gasping and very relieved.

'Captain Buckett!' I straightened my hair and my clothes simultaneously as the smuggler captain held what seemed like a huge pistol to the head of my David. 'There is no need for that!'

'Mayhap there is not and mayhap there is,' Buckett did not remove the muzzle of his pistol from David's temple. 'Your mother asked me to keep an eye on you, Miss Sarah and I saw this lobster leading you into the chapel. Just say the word and I'll decorate the walls with his brains.'

Well, as you can imagine, that offer did not tempt me in the least. I mean, David and I were to be married after all and men do get carried away with themselves sometime. They cannot help it, you see, especially in the presence of a pretty girl as I was. Or so I believed at the time. We do, you know; we give that sort of man far too much leeway and then wonder why so many of us fall into disgrace. Well, ladies, if you are reading my tale, then take a hint from me and don't be attracted to men who attempt to take liberties with you. If you do not wish their attentions, then say so firmly and directly. If they withdraw at once, then they are gentleman, whatever their social standing, and there is hope for them. If they do not withdraw then a swift and hard kick in a very private place is a nearly certain cure, and if you cannot do that, then arrange to have a sturdy smuggling captain standing by with a large pistol.

'I am sorry,' David proved the truth of my words by dropping his hands and being immediately contrite. The presence of a pistol at his head may have influenced his actions. 'I really don't know what came over me.'

At any rate I was prepared to forgive and nearly forget, so I accepted his apology at once and proffered my cheek for a chaste kiss.

'There will be plenty of time for such antics after we are married,' I told him comfortably as James Buckett uncocked his pistol and withdrew a step or two. The circular imprint of the muzzle on David's temple was a suitable reminder, and one that I did not offer to ease with a kiss. I was, I admit, slightly shaken by the whole affair.

'If that is all you are after,' James Buckett spoke to David from the door, 'I am sure I can find you a whore suitable for your needs.' He remained within the chapel, watching us both.

'Captain Buckett!' I admonished him. 'There is no need for such foc's'le language within a church. I am surprised at you.' I had heard worse of course; working in an inn with smugglers and foremast hands, one tends to hear a whole range of colourful and expressive language. Sometimes it gave me quite a thrill to hear the phrases men would use and I had quite a number of expressions saved up for any possible argument with my future husband, whoever he happened to be. At that time I thought it would be David, of course, and I was quite resolved to give him a very vivid talking-to on some future occasion when I was secure in our marriage and he had made some fault or other. Men need such a forthright woman, you see. The milk-and-water simpering type of wife will not be a helpmate to a real man.

Buckett took no heed of my strictures. Presumably his own wife addressed him in such terms, or was even more rigorous in her words and actions.

'Lieutenant Baldivere,' Buckett's voice was low and gruff as any fighting dog. 'If I see you, or hear of you, treating Miss Bembridge in any manner other than that of a gentleman, I will take you out to sea and drop you overboard with a brace of thirty-two-pound cannonballs tied to each of your ankles.'

'I assure you, sir...' Poor David began, until he realised that he was talking to an open door. Buckett had left without another word.

Well, Buckett's little intervention rather dampened David's ardour and my enthusiasm for showing him more of the estate, so we returned to the Horse Head. The day had not quite gone as I had hoped, really. Still it could have been worse and I had the memory of a kiss or two.

Chapter Ten

'Sarah!' Mother knew no other name save mine that morning. I scurried back downstairs, mop in hand and perspiration on brow.

'Yes, Mother?'

'Get you along to Mrs Downer in Chale. Ask her if she has any more chickens ready for us yet.' Mother gave me her most venomous glare, 'well move then, girl: what are you standing there for?'

Leaving the mop and bucket behind the counter, I picked up my travelling cloak and fled. It was something of a relief to get away from Mother's harping voice that morning, and I breathed deeply of the bright air the second I stepped outside.

The air was crisp with a cheerful bite that reminded of the past winter and made it good to be alive. Chale is our nearest village, a short stroll along the road, but Mrs Downer lived in a cottage all by itself a few minutes' walk to the westward.

I banged the inn door shut to express my displeasure at being treated like a skivvy, set my shoulders to prove I was in a monumental huff, lifted my skirt free from the worst of the dew on the grass and set out quite happily toward Chale. If that sounds like a bit of an oxymoron, remember that I was very young and there is nothing that pleases a young girl more than to be at the centre of a piece of drama. I resolved to keep my Monday face on as long as I could, and seek sympathy for my sorrows.

You may know the south coast of the Island of course, so there is probably no need for me to tell you of the long beach of Chale Bay that stretches forever to the west and north, joining with Brighstone Bay and with the great chalk cliffs with their bird-life and groups of vivid wild flowers, while in the far distance thrust the spectacular headland of the Needles that the sailors use as a seamark. Although I was born and bred on the island, the sheer loveliness of it all still takes my breath away so my eyes swivelled this way and that, enjoying everything, as I always did, despite my mother's constant assertion that I was just wasting my time in so doing.

I passed the straggle of cottages that was Chale and hurried onto the grass grown path that led down to Mrs Downer's cottage, just at the head of Whale Chine. Mrs Downer was outside in her garden, hoeing her newly planted vegetables for we all needed to grow what we could in case Boney stole them all overnight.

'Ah, Sarah,' she greeted me with a smile that always made me feel better, however downcast my mood. 'Your mother will be asking about the chickens then?'

I wondered, as I had so often before, how Mrs Downer knew exactly what I was about to say. I nodded and her eyes twinkled as she drew the back of her hand across her forehead, leaving a broad grimy band. 'Pray tell her that I can supply a dozen at once, or one at a time for as long as she likes, provided that she sends somebody to pick them up.' She pointed her hoe at me. 'That will mean you, of course!'

I nodded. 'I suppose it will.'

Mrs Downer looked closer at me. 'You are a bit disconsolate this morning,' she said. 'I can't think why. It's a beautiful day, the sun is shining and there are all sorts of interesting things happening in the world.' She stopped there and looked at me, smiling with just her eyes, and I just had to ask for more details.

'What sort of interesting things are happening?'

'Oh all sorts.' Mrs Downer returned to her hoeing, scraping the metal end over the soil to kill off any weeds that might have escaped her earlier attention. 'You have that lieutenant in tow and are due to be married; that is surely of interest.'

I nodded, for that thought was always in the forefront of my mind. 'I am nearly a married woman,' I blurted out in my anger, 'and Mother insists on treating me as if I was still her kitchen maid.'

'Mothers do these things,' Mrs Downer said with a smile, 'and they give nothing in return except endless love, a room, board, keep, training for life and lots of free advice.' She allowed me to ponder her words for a moment and then changed the subject.

'As well as your intended husband and your cruel mother, the world has other things to offer.' She nodded out to sea. 'There is that sloop out there patrolling for smugglers or French privateers, and the convoy on the horizon on its way to London, and all these men who were using the coastal road this morning and not a fear of the Press in any of them.'

'All which men?' My interest was aroused, as Mrs Downer had intended, the cunning witch. She looked at me through her shrewd eyes. 'There was that travelling fellow first: the man who is staying at your Inn, and then...'

'Mr Howard?' I burst in, rudely.

'Is that what he calls himself?' Mrs Downer looked surprised although I am certain she knew Mr Howard's name, place of birth and antecedents all the way back to Adam and Eve. 'Well then, Mr Howard it was. And a few minutes later came a patrol of Volunteers, shambling along with their muskets over their shoulders and chewing baccy as if they had never heard of Napoleon Bonaparte and the French.'

I looked along the coastal path. It was empty just now as far as I could see. Limestone Manor was clearly visible in the middle distance, just past the rocks of Atherfield Point and before Shepherd's Chine.

'Could I catch Mr Howard?' I asked hopefully.

Mrs Downer shook her head. 'Not unless you grew wings, Sarah. Your Mr Howard was on horseback. A fine brown mare.' She looked at me and smiled. 'I thought you might find all these comings and goings of interest. You do like to know what is going on and nobody bothers if an old biddy like me sees them. Us oldsters are invisible you know; we are only part of the landscape, like the trees.'

I said nothing to that, but I recognised that Mrs Downer was hinting at my natural inquisitiveness. I looked again at the path to Limestone Manor.

'Was your mother in a hurry to find out about the chickens?' Mrs Downer asked with as much innocence as a hunting viper.

'I don't know,' I replied, truthfully.

'Did she tell you to hurry back?' Mrs Downer dripped her questions subtly.

I shook my head and Mrs Downer returned to her hoeing. 'It's only two miles to Limestone Manor,' she mumbled, placed her hoe against the hedge and walked straight-backed, toward her cottage. She halted at the door and looked back at me, her eyes bright and old and wise. 'That was where Mr Howard was heading, you know.' She closed the door.

Two miles on a glorious morning is always a pleasure. Temporarily forgetting to sulk, my mother's cantankerous mood and the errand on which I had been sent, I lifted my skirt and skipped along the road. I was fully aware, of course, that I was being very foolish in doing so, but I did not care, and that was unusual for me. I normally care a great deal, as you will know by now, but for some reason I did not yet understand, I was feeling suddenly free and flighty and irresponsible. I love the sensation of a fresh breeze through my hair, and the sound of the breakers hushing along the beach at Chale Bay is sweeter than choral music, but even so my heart was hammering as I approached the wall and hedge and rusted iron gates that marked the boundary of Limestone Manor.

I stopped there. Everything was the same as always. The wall was as tumbledown as ever, with the coping stones all a-crumble where stray animals had kicked at them; the hedge was an explosion of briars and brambles, alive with honey bees and swaying slightly in the onshore breeze. But the gate was open. Now I was twenty years old and had lived in the Back of Wight all my life and I had never seen that gate open before. That in itself was worthy of my attention.

I walked the last few steps slowly, nearly afraid to get too close. These gates were eighteen feet high and had once been beautiful. They were of wrought iron and sat between two stone pillars, each augmented by a carved elephant standing on its hind legs. Salt air from the sea had corroded each iron railing and the elephants were green with moss, so they looked as if they had a fur coat that suited them not one whit. I looked inside the estate, peered up the once graceful driveway that swept to an unseen front door and wondered if I should enter.

Of course I should. I was a local here, a Caulkhead: this was my island! I squared my shoulders, straightened my back and marched straight in, as erect as any guardsman marching to face the French. Except that it was hard to march while advancing along a driveway that had been invaded and conquered by a million weeds that rose knee high; and where moles had tunnelled under the ground so I wobbled on my boots and swayed uncertainly. I stopped at a patch of soft ground; there, in plain sight, was the imprint of a horse's hoof. I knelt down; the earth at the side of the print was barely crumbling so it had been recently made. It seemed obvious to me that Mr Howard had opened the front gate and had passed this way. I stood up and followed the curve of the path in momentary expectation of seeing Mr Howard with his worn cloak and slashed tricorne hat. I turned a corner and there it was: Limestone Manor: I stopped short and stared.

I do not know what I expected but I knew what I was looking at should have been the house of a gentleman of means. It was old, perhaps centuries old, with great wide windows and tall chimneys. It was huge; larger by far than any house in the vicinity and twice as large as Knighton Hazard. The architecture was beautiful but, unfortunately, Limestone Manor was also a derelict wreck. The panes of nearly all the windows were smashed so they gaped like sightless eyes from the face of a house bereft of a soul. At some point a Channel gale had brought two of the chimneys crashing down, one to strew shattered brickwork across what had once been a well-tended lawn, the other to tear a ragged hole in the slates of the roof and do who-knew-what damage to the interior of the house. There was a rookery in a copse of trees beside the coach house and the raucous caws of the inhabitants were an ugly backdrop to the dereliction of what had been a well-loved home.

I stared at Limestone Manor, fascinated by the obvious wealth and power that had once been here while still dismayed by the ruin of such a magnificent building. But for the life of me I could not understand why Mr Howard or anybody else would want to come here. There was nothing except a crumbling ruin, tangled grounds and a host of evil stories that were certainly exaggerations and possibly downright lies.

Now I was so close, my natural inquisitive nature would not allow me to back off. Keeping as quiet as I could on the weed-infested gravel walkway that extended around the house, I stepped to the main entrance. The house faced the sea, with a flight of stone steps soaring to a front door so grand I could imagine the Governor of Wight, nobility and even royalty arriving there in a convoy of golden carriages. A tangle of nettles partly obscured the neo-classical portico with the soaring fluted pillars that guarded the iron studded door, but when I ascended up the steps it was locked as securely as the Bank of England on a Sunday.

I pushed as hard as I was able but the door remained obstinately shut; it was obvious that if Mr Howard was inside he had ensured that nobody could follow him. With a mixture of disappointment and relief, I turned away and began to retrace my steps, now anxious to get away from this closed place. I was moving at some speed, with my legs snapping against the constriction of my skirt when I heard the voices. I nearly used the foremast hand's foul language, looked desperately around and slipped into the angle between the stairs and the house so I would not be seen. Now, you may think it strange that I thought to hide myself, for I was a free-born Englishwoman and was breaking no law, but in that wary year of 1803 we were all on edge in case Johnny Crapaud would invade. Wight has a history of French invasion, being an island close to the coast of the continent, so we slept uneasy in our beds at that time.

I was right to hide, for the voices were of strangers and the language was indeed French. I cowered into the corner, feeling the cold bite of stone pressing hard against my back and other places, and wished I had resisted the temptation to enter those gates. It was too late now: I was well and truly trapped. The voices came closer; three of them, two men and a woman, talking openly and loudly as if they owned the place. I felt my temper rise; the cheek of them, wandering around so blatantly as if Admiral Duncan had not stopped their invasion attempt only a few years back and as if Admiral Nelson did not exist!

I shrunk myself as small as I could as the French approached, their voices jabbering above the crunch of feet on the gravel. I expected to smell garlic and onions but instead there was just a whiff of tobacco. They passed me without looking round: the woman was around forty years old, strikingly good looking with a proud, erect carriage and a way of walking that seemed to make her glide across the ground. I compared her grace to my own country gait and resolved that in future I would beat the French at their own elegant game.

The first man was stocky with a mobile face that could have been handsome if he had not been French, and the second man wore a very familiar tricorne hat with a badly stitched cut. I nearly screamed as I realised that it was Mr Howard.

Did that mean that Mr Howard was a French spy? Was my island already over-run with people from that blasted nation?

They walked right past me and around the corner of the house, with Mr Howard and the woman speaking in animated French and the stocky man puffing aromatic tobacco smoke into the air like some fiend from the Republican Pit. None of them so much as glanced in my direction, and after they I had gone I felt such a wave of rage toward them that rather than lift up my skirt and run, which would have been the sensible thing to do, I followed after them, pausing at the corner of the house to ensure they were not waiting to trap me.

They were not. I rounded the corner just in time to see Mr Howard politely hold open a side door for the woman to step through. He glanced around but must have failed to see me for he followed the woman inside. I allowed them a few moments and tiptoed in their wake, trying to make no noise on the shifting gravel. Why did I follow, you may wonder, when they were obviously French and I could be in very grave danger? Well you must remember the spirit of the time when we all lived in fear of the French so the thought of them boldly walking about my island made my blood boil. The fact that I was also inquisitive, and still am, had nothing whatever to do with it, I assure you. Or perhaps just a tiny little bit.

The side door was set in a small round tower on the extreme south western corner of the house. It swung slightly ajar as I turned the handle and I looked into the darkness inside. The smell of damp and decay slammed into me so I gagged, backed off a pace, settled my mind and returned. I wrapped my shawl around my mouth and nose and stepped into the unknown. I really am a slave to my curiosity you see; that and my dislike of Johnny Crapaud.

I felt my way inch by inch into a small, stone flagged square and onto a circular stair case that led upward to a landing. As though embarrassed to illuminate such a dismal place, the light that filtered reluctantly through layers of cobwebs in a tiny window was grey yet still revealed four doors, each one leading in a different direction. With my heart pounding, yet too long-nosed to withdraw, I tried each in turn; only one opened, its hinges creaking so loudly that I was sure the whole of the Back of the Wight would hear.

I stopped for a heart-stopping moment, expecting half of France to burst out of the door to attack me. Instead there was silence save for a slight scratching that could have come from a rat or a bird. I took a deep breath and stepped into a corridor that led into a darkness that wrapped around me like a cloak.

You may wonder at my courage. Well I will tell you that I am not so much courageous as plain pig-headed. It is a trait that has got me into more trouble than you may ever imagine. Take some free advice from me and keep your head secure on your shoulders and your thoughts locked inside your head. Use your brain and think what you do, as I most certainly did not.

The voices came as a low grumble, interspaced with the high clear tones of that woman. I listened for a few moments, wishing that I could speak French so I could understand what was being said, and then as my eyes grew accustomed to the dark I realised that there was a line of shifting light under a door in the corridor, a sure sign that the room was occupied and illuminated.

Lifting my skirt above my ankles, I stepped forward cautiously, just as the door swung slowly toward me. I gasped in fear and shrunk back into the providential shelter of a recessed doorway.

For a moment I could see inside the room. Mr Howard, that mobile faced man and the oh-so-elegant woman were grouped around a table. However I was so intent on inspecting the people that I nearly forgot to look at the other interesting things in that concealed room. By the time the door was swinging shut again my view was constrained so I may well have missed sight of something important. What I did see convinced me that there was bad work afoot and something would have to be done about it.

There was a single lantern hanging from a hook on the wall, pooling yellow light and shadows across a battered circular oak table. The two men and one woman sat around a map of southern England, with little wooden ships sitting on the sea in between, for all the world like children's toys on a nursery floor. Central to the map was our own island of Wight, with the bows of three of the little wooden ships pointed directly toward the very bay in which I lived.

If anybody had been able to see me, they would have had an amazingly clear view of my tonsils, my mouth was so wide. I closed it with a click, at exactly the same time as somebody within the room pulled shut their door.

I had seen enough. There was absolutely no doubt in my mind that our Mr Howard was either French or was working with them, and they intended to land some sort of force in Wight. I should have been angry, even frightened, but instead my mind was on the three people who had sat around that circular table. That woman had moved with more grace than any hunting cat: I wanted to emulate her style. The mobile faced man had total control of himself; he was obviously a man of some authority, while his looks suggested that he walked on the dark side of the street. Yet both faded into insignificance beside Mr Howard. I could think of little save his less-than-handsome face and duplicity of character as I hurried back along the bay to Mother.

I did not tell her of my little adventure. I had too much in my mind to share with anybody. I could only wrestle with the images and wish that I knew what to do and who to tell.

The answer to that was obvious. I was soon to be married and who better to tell than my own handsome, passionate David? I resolved that once the wedding festivities were complete, I would tell him all. With that settled in my mind, I tried to forget elegant French women, monkey-faced French men and especially Mr Howard, and concentrate on my own handsome lieutenant of Volunteers.

Chapter Eleven

The mist returned that afternoon, thickening as it ghosted in from the Channel until by night-time it was a real pea-souper and our customers came in hunched and dripping, to take off their hats and beat them dry against the flanks of their coats or the legs of their breeches and complain about the weather. Of course after enduring the fog they needed something to fortify them and my mother was always willing to oblige.

There were a dozen men and not many less women clustered in the tap room when Mr Howard entered and not a single one stopped to even offer him a nod. Well, I knew he was a Frenchman and therefore an enemy of our blood and as such should be hanged or shot or otherwise disposed of, but that was no excuse for downright rudeness.

'Good evening Mr Howard,' I called out, as cheerily as I ever could even as I scanned him for evidence of his French-ness. I found none and thought that these French spies are very good at appearing English.

'Good evening Sarah, my dear,' he replied with as amiable a smile as one could hope for from a Frenchman. I smiled back of course, and wished that I could tell everybody what I knew without getting myself into trouble.

That's the worst thing about being slightly inquisitive, you know, one gets oneself into all temperatures of water from hot to utterly unbearable. The other not-good thing is that when one ferrets out secrets, one cannot tell anybody about them without disclosing how they were obtained. When I was younger and foolish I used to broadcast my findings to Mother or to Kitty. I do not advise that anybody follows that course of action, I really don't. Mother took instant action that I do not wish to recount while Kitty proved utterly incapable of keeping even the most delicious of secrets. I lost many good friends when

Kitty related to them what I had told her about their actions, although I had always told Kitty in the strictest of confidence.

So I kept my knowledge to myself and set about being the most amiable of hosts for the despicable Mr Howard.

'You are alone, I see,' I opened the conversation with something innocent.

'You have good eyesight,' replied my secretive companion.

I smiled at his compliment. 'Thank you, sir,' I gave a little curtsey as the female I had seen him with must have often done to him. I had resolved to be more refined, you must remember, and to equal if not surpass the elegance of that pestilent Frenchwoman.

Mr Howard asked what was on the menu and Mother bustled up to take over, ordering me away to serve another table where a group of local men, brown-faced yokels with dirt under their fingernails and absolutely no refinement, were scooping mutton and gravy into their mouths as if they were pigs at the trough. Honestly! After mingling with gentleman such as my lieutenant and Mr Howard I knew I was destined for far better things than serving such people. But needs must when the devil drives the coach so I took their orders and banged down tankards of ale for them to quaff, accepted their dirty coppers and watched Mr Howard over my shoulder the whole time.

'He's still here, then,' I had not noticed Mrs Downer arrive.

'Who?' I asked in pretended innocence.

'That man you followed this morning.' Mrs Downer did not lower her tone. I waved my hand frantically to her, fearful in case Mother or, indeed, Mr Howard, should hear.

'I did not follow any man,' I denied stoutly.

'I see,' Mrs Downer's wink transformed her face from that of an old woman to that of a hideous hag that would haunt the nightmares of even the most wicked of children. Her cackle was worse as I silently begged her to be more circumspect and dreaded that Mr Howard should hear her imputations.

Molly came in, her eyes as wise as any night owl, and I nearly ran to her table, desperate for a friend in whom I could confide.

'It's all right,' Molly lifted her hands before I had the chance to speak. 'He is in good hands.'

'Who?' Of course my first thought was of Mr Howard, and then, a trifle guiltily, of David. Eventually I worked out that Molly was referring to my

French sailor, whose presence I had all but forgotten in all the excitement. 'Oh good,' I said with a forced smile. 'I was worried about him.'

'So I see,' Molly said.

'How is his poor head?' I asked, 'and his poor ankle?'

'His poor head is still bruised; probably more so after your good friend Kitty threw him on the floor, while we will not know about his poor ankle until he is conscious and tries to use it.'

I had to answer the demands of a crew of fishermen then, fresh in from the sea and smelling of fish and sweat and the honest briny. Once that was done I saw Molly laughing with Mr Howard and decided not to interfere. I had much too much in my mind and nobody in which to confide. Keeping secrets is not for the faint-hearted you see. It is far better to tell somebody everything. I mean, I am always ready to listen if you wish to tell me … but that night I was not able to confide. If I had I may have saved myself some trouble.

Chapter Twelve

The chapel was crowded for my first wedding, which went off splendidly up to a point. All was exactly as I had imagined. The pews were packed with people, with one side filled with the scarlet and gold of the Volunteers, mainly officers of course but a few of the more respectable sergeants and what-nots, with a brace of stalwart privates standing sentinel at the door. There was even a scattering of officer's wives, in gowns that would have cost as much to buy as the Horse Head, and faces that refused to smile or even acknowledge the existence of those on the other side of the central aisle. I paid particular attention to these wives of course, for in a very few moments I would be of their ilk, and I smiled to them from my position at the altar. A few nearly thought about returning the compliment while others could not have noticed, or were too preoccupied with their own business to respond to me. Captain Chadwick, the aloof commander of the Volunteers, proved my earlier perceptions incorrect as he greeted me with a friendly nod and had his men stand the moment I entered the chapel.

On the other side of the dividing aisle were my own people, the Caulkheads of the Back of Wight. Mother sat at the front, flanked by Kitty and her mother, Katie Chillerton, all in their Sunday best and with Mother dashing away a tear from her eye as she looked at me. I thought then that she must have borrowed it from a passing crocodile. With my father still a-voyaging or perhaps a prisoner of the French, Mother asked John Nash to give me away, which he did with gruff aplomb and a kind of natural grace that made me wonder if my own father had been like him. Hugo Bertram had taken a prime position in the Caulkhead side of the congregation, standing proud yet alone as he surveyed all these visitors to his chapel.

More importantly, he gave me a broad grin and a nod of approval as I stepped up to the altar.

I know that the day of a girl's marriage is supposed to be the best day of her life, the end of her girlhood and the beginning of womanhood. I am not sure if my first wedding day was like that. I was in such a dream that I barely remember the ceremony at all.

The Reverend Barwis was there, with his robes and Holy Book, and I expect that he made us repeat certain words and phrases but for the life of me I could not tell you what I said. I do remember that David looked very handsome in his scarlet uniform and smiled down on me as we stood side by side in front of the assembled congregation.

I also remember the Reverend Barwis saying: 'you may kiss the bride' and David doing so, not in any great burst of passion as he had done last time we were in this same place, but with dignity and decorum, as befitted an officer, a gentleman and a married man.

Strangely, it was Captain Chadwick who was first to congratulate me as he bowed and offered me his hand, and then a whole host of people were there, from Hugo Bertram to John Nash and two of the officers' wives who were distant but polite. I revelled in the attention, being very condescending to those of my friends who were not fortunate enough to be married to a Volunteer officer, and very attentive to those new friends who were.

Kitty came last, pressing up close to me with the light of mischief in her eyes and a deep chuckle in her throat.

'You can tell me all about tonight later,' she said.

'Don't be so crude,' I admonished her. 'What happens between a husband and wife is private.'

Kitty's laugh was anything but private. 'Even to your closest and most amiable friend?'

I could not help but smile. Kitty and I have shared all our secrets since childhood. 'Only if you solemnly swear not to tell another living soul.' I said.

She nodded, straight faced and sincere as only the very best of prevaricators could be. 'You know I would never do that,' she said.

'I'll call on you as soon as I can,' I said, for in truth I was rather looking forward to giving her every last detail so the little minx squirmed in jealousy as I, the wife of a Volunteer officer, treated her to tales that she, a known wanton, could never hope to emulate. I was now a woman of position while she could merely hang on my coat tails and hope for crumbs from my table, if I chose to give her any.

We filed outside into a glorious day of warm sunshine, with the Channel as blue as you could wish and spangled with the sails of a score of ships. I stood there with David on my arm and the future bright before us. For one glorious, happy moment married life was good, but that was the only flicker of time that fate afforded us.

I could not see the future then, or the darkness that the corporal carried as he ran through the gate of the churchyard to deliver his message to Captain Chadwick. There is an old saying, 'don't shoot the messenger' but if I had possessed a pistol that day, and the means to look into our immediate future, I would have aimed it at that gasping corporal and shot him, bang, right between the eyes. But I had not and he still lives, no doubt as happily as a corporal can live with a corporal's wife and a host of little corporal children, each with two corporal stripes on his or her arm … but I digress and who can blame me?

'Sir,' that corporal said as he saluted. I can see him now, with his clean-shaven face and narrow blue eyes. 'Sir, begging your pardon for interrupting the wedding sir, but Lieutenant Compton sends his compliments sir, and a whole section has deserted, sir and could you help search this end of the island, sir.'

Somehow I knew there would be trouble after that message with its plethora of sirs.

'The devil, you say?' Captain Chadwick's commented, somewhat incoherently. 'An entire section deserted? We can't have that!' He looked around the churchyard, into which his officers were slowly filing, talking to each other and to their wives, quite happy and relaxed. 'Volunteers!' He said in an impressively commanding voice, 'form up!'

After a short hesitation, due to surprise I presume, they obeyed at once, officers and men rushing to form three short lines in front of him in front of the chapel.

'I am sorry to break up such a happy gathering,' Captain Chadwick said, 'but Corporal Nickerson has brought me the gravest tidings.'

I saw some of the wives look alarmed and one asked openly if Boney had landed. The Volunteers stiffened further at that suggestion.

'It is worse than that,' Captain Chadwick said. 'I have had news that an entire section of Volunteers, our men, have proved disloyal to their sworn oath and have deserted the regiment.'

There were gasps of disbelief from the wives and stern looks from the officers. My own husband looked at me with the most severe expression on his countenance. I was all a-flutter myself, wondering what on earth would happen next.

'All officers and men, without exception, will report to Horseshoe Bay in Ventnor and we will scour the island for these unfaithful devils.'

As the officers began to bark orders, Captain Chadwick approached me. 'I am very sorry to take your husband away from you on this most special of days,' he said, 'but the duties of the service must always come first. I am sure you understand.'

'Of course, sir,' I said, thinking that the Captain was not at all an ogre and looked quite splendid in his uniform. He was a most dignified man, you see, and unmarried, poor soul. All good men need a wife to keep them safe from temptation, as I am sure I have already said.

Captain Chadwick bowed. 'I will send him back to you as soon as I am able. You will both continue to stay at the Horse Head until the regiment moves to Dublin?'

'Yes, sir,' I said.

He nodded. 'There is no need to call me sir when we are alone, my dear. You are part of the Regiment now. My given name is William.'

With that final kindness he was gone, leaving me temporarily bereft of a husband, and my arrangements for a wedding breakfast in the Horse Head all in tatters. Of course Mother was never at a loss and packed up all the spare food to be used at a later date while the women and those men who remained made a good job of demolishing the ale and wines.

'You may have to spend the night alone after all,' Kitty consoled me with a hug. 'Unless you wish me to find a suitable bed mate? There are many men who could take poor David's place if need be.'

I knew she was trying to make light of my situation to make me feel better, yet I still responded with a burst of ill-temper that included many of the colourful words that I had learned from the fishermen and smugglers. Kitty withdrew with her face as scarlet as any Volunteer uniform and I slunk to a corner of the tap-room to console myself with a brandy or two. It may not be a drink thought suitable for ladies but at times only the strongest of spirits can help revive a flagging spirit.

I heard the popping of musketry without interest. It could have been any regiment training or even men after a rabbit or a bird of prey, yet my mother raised her head in concern and looked over to me.

'You had better be about some work,' she said, which was her answer to anything, good or bad, 'rather than sitting there brooding.'

'I am not brooding,' I said, lifting my third glass of brandy to my lips. 'I am waiting for my husband to come home.'

I did not have long to wait. Within the hour there was a knock at the door which Mother answered, and then half a dozen Volunteers trooped in. They looked at me with pale, unhappy faces and spoke to each other in low voices.

'What's happened? What's the matter?' I asked, and then, knowing that something was wrong, I added, 'where's my husband?'

Mother came to me with her mouth set. 'It will be all right,' she said, 'it will all be all right,' and she pulled me close in a very unaccustomed hug. I knew then that it was very much not all right. I knew then that David was dead.

Four more of the Volunteers arrived, bearing the body of David on a makeshift litter. They laid him down on one of the tables and looked to me.

'I am very sorry for your loss,' Captain Chadwick said. 'He was a fine man and a promising young officer.'

I looked down upon my husband. There were two bullet holes in him; one in the centre of his forehead and the other in the centre of his chest. 'They have spoiled his dress coat,' was all that I could say, while my heart was breaking within me and my mind was numb.

At such times, people do not know how to react. The full horror had not come to me yet. I only knew that I was a widow without ever having known the joys of being a wife.

'We will give him a full military funeral,' Captain Chadwick promised, as if that was of any consolation at all.

'What happened?' I know I asked that, although my voice did not seem to belong to me. It was as if I floated above my body, watching some stranger go through the motions of life while being utterly detached from the awful reality.

'We were hunting for the deserters,' Captain Chadwick said. 'They did not want to be arrested and shot at us. Poor Lieutenant Baldivere was leading his men.'

'They murdered him.' I said, standing up. I felt such anger then that I could not control what I said next. 'I want them hanged. I want to see them swinging at the end of a rope.'

But I did not really. I was angry beyond words, yet I had no notion to inflict this pain of bereavement on any other person. I remembered that the privates had been forced into uniform. In a way, I think I began to grow up then, with the body of my husband before me and his blood drying on the uniform. I was not mature yet, that I know, but I had taken the first step.

'They are already dead,' Captain Chadwick said. 'Justice has been done.'

I nodded. I did not cry; there were not enough tears in the world to wash away what I was feeling. Without a word, I stood up and blundered out of the Horse Head Inn and over the downland to the Long Stone. It was there, where David and I had been so happy, that I released my grief and it was there, hours later, that Molly and my mother found me, still weeping, and brought me home.

Chapter Thirteen

I will not spend much time over the next few weeks of that eventful year. There is sufficient grief and mourning in everybody's life without forcing you to read of it in a book that is supposed to be about romance. Suffice it to say that it was not the best period in my young life and I was supported by true friends both old and new.

My mother was always there, keeping me busy, and so was Kitty, strangely enough. Molly gave advice and support while Captain Chadwick and Mr Howard hovered in the background, the latter as a father figure for all his French connection and the former as something else, although I did not yet know quite what, then.

We buried David in the graveyard that wrapped somberly around the parish church with all the officers standing in silent mourning and most of the people of the parish bare-headed and quiet as they tried to avoid my eyes while still expressing genuine sympathy. Whoever knows what to say at a funeral? That was a silent day of grey mist and I will not dwell on it. I am not one to reminisce over bad times; they were there, they were horrible and then they passed. Let us just say that I survived them and learned a lesson or two. Not enough to come out as a mature, thinking woman, yet enough to wave farewell to a lot of the flighty foolishness of that young girl about whom I have been writing so far in this story of mine.

You may think that I spent the entire next few weeks in mourning for my departed love. Well that was not what happened. My mother and Molly both allowed me a couple of days to myself and then they urged me into toilsome activity.

'I hope you don't expect me to run the inn on my own and look after you,' Mother put on her most severe tone, 'and working is the best way you can get back to being yourself again.'

'You rescued that poor man from the sea,' Molly added her two-penny worth. 'Now you are responsible for looking after him.'

Between the two of them I was sent from the inn to Molly's house, from skivvy to nurse, from barmaid to helper so that when I eventually got to bed I slept the sleep of the totally exhausted and although the pain was still there, the absolute bewilderment of loss was diminishing. My Frenchman had minutes of lucidity and times when he was completely comatose. Sometimes he spoke in French and at other times in English, yet he was never forthcoming with his name or anything else we could use to identify him.

'Now, try and walk,' I said on one of the times he was awake.

He took my hand willingly enough and fell in quite a spectacular fashion as soon as I guided him out of bed.

Molly helped me put him back in between the covers, where he promptly lost consciousness once more. My failure to help my pet Frenchman combined with the loss of David to dull my normally cheerful disposition so I snapped at Kitty when she came along to see how I was doing.

'I miss David,' I said.

'It's not as if you were in love with him,' Kitty said, tactfully. 'You only wanted the position and the glamour of his uniform.'

There was some truth in that. There was also truth in James Buckett's observation a few weeks after the death.

'He was a handsome enough fellow,' Buckett said. 'That I will allow. Yet he was not a good man. No good man treats a lady the way he treated you that time I found him with you. If he was like that before you married, mark my words, he would be worse afterward, when you were both behind closed doors.' He gave a twisted grin. 'I am glad he was shot. It saved me the trouble.'

I took a deep breath. 'Why would you do that for me?'

'Your father is a good man,' Buckett said. 'He would want me to look after his daughter until he gets home.'

That surprised me. I had always looked on Buckett as a wild, uncouth man with neither morals nor scruples. Now I saw him in a different light, and also saw that side of David that I had conveniently pushed to the back of my mind.

While I was mulling over these facts, I realised that all the time I was re-covering from my recent widowhood; Captain Chadwick had become a very frequent visitor to the Horse Head. At first he merely asked how I was and bought himself a glass of French brandy, but on his third or fourth visit he asked if he could speak to me privately.

I agreed of course. It was quite flattering to have a captain of Volunteers paying so much court to me. I could feel Mother watching from behind the counter, and Captain Nash looked up briefly from a discussion with Buckett, frowned and looked away. I was not sure if I liked so many middle aged men taking an interest in my affairs, yet I said nothing.

'Miss Bembridge,' Captain Chadwick had a deeper voice that David, and I thought the lines of experience around his eyes and mouth were quite distinguished, 'I am very distraught that it was an order of mine that sent your husband to such an unfortunate occurrence.'

I was not sure how to react to that. I had not forgotten David, of course, yet for all my despondency I was pragmatic enough to realise that his death was in the past, I was young and the world had many interests for me other than a deceased lieutenant in the Volunteers. I think I only smiled to the caring captain.

'I would dearly like to make it up to you in some way, Miss Bembridge.' Captain Chadwick continued.

'I am sure it was not your fault,' I told him. 'My husband died doing his duty.'

The captain nodded. 'You would be an excellent wife to any Volunteer officer,' Captain Chadwick said, 'whatever his rank.'

It was only then that I realised the captain was intending more than mere friendship. I may have gasped; I know that I stared at him. Now you may think badly of me but please remember I was a very young girl and we were involved in a very ugly and prolonged war. It was also true that living by the sea we were used to death, with seamen and fishermen risking their lives on a daily basis even without the threat of war, so there were many widows in the Back of Wight and I had seen more than a few women married while their widow's weeds were still fresh from the maker. My own position was only slightly different because of the length of time I had been married.

After that day, Captain Chadwick became an ever more frequent visitor to the Horse Head and although he was never impolite to Mother, he always danced attendance on me. He never stated his intentions openly, merely asking for my welfare, chatting a little and smiling a lot.

I basked in his attention without ever taking him seriously as I recovered from my period of mourning and continued with my own life. After all, what could a captain of Volunteers see in a widowed inn-keeper's daughter?

It was two weeks later that Captain Chadwick approached my mother with a most serious expression on his face and asked to speak to her alone. I was so naïve that I thought I had offended him in some way, perhaps by giving him the wrong meal or short-changing him as he paid for the brandy. Mother must have thought the same for she gave me the most peculiar look as she ushered Captain Chadwick to the small room in the back where she conducted all her private business.

I would have drifted to the door to listen in to the conversation, as was my wont, but the tap-room was busy and I had to serve my customers. Mr Howard was particularly attentive at that time and pressed me for information regarding my state of mind and intentions for the future.

'Well now Sarah, you are looking worried today.' Mr Howard said, putting one hand on my arm and smiling most benignly. 'You have had a troubling time, recently.'

I agreed, yet could not pay him my full attention, French agent although he was. I had a strange feeling that I should offer to re-stitch his hat; he seemed in great need of feminine attention of that sort.

'I know it is too early to think of such things,' Mr Howard said, 'but don't despair too much my dear; there will be another man to care for you soon.'

I cannot recall exactly what I told him; probably the usual platitudes one uses with older men. I may have told him that it was women who cared for men rather than vice versa; I hope so for that is the truth. I mean: just you compare single women with single men. The women are far more often self-reliant, sober and industrious while the men tend to frequent the inns, keeping Mother in funds, and walk about unkempt, unshaven and unhappy.

I am sure I smiled as best I could and thanked Mr Howard for his solicitations, while hoping that he did not include himself in the list of eligible men who were apparently queuing up to rescue me from the horrors of a man-free existence. I can recall the expression of incredulity on Mr Howard's face when Mother and Captain Chadwick emerged from Mother's little den.

'Sarah Baldivere!' Mother said. She had got into the habit of calling me that to remind me of my new status as a recent widow, although the marriage had never been consummated.

'Yes, Mother,' I said at once, waiting for her harpy-tongue to condemn me for some fault of omission or commission.

'Captain Chadwick has asked my permission to seek your hand in marriage. Do you consent?'

'Oh dear God,' I said, staring at my latest suitor as the tap-room suddenly hushed and Mr Howard dropped his fork with a clatter that seemed to echo for ever.

Chapter Fourteen

Now, I hope that you will forgive me if I leave that situation where it was and explain what else was happening in my life. You see, however intense my romantic existence, I was also still occupied in looking after my slowly recovering Frenchman. I walked to Molly's house every day with a basket of food from the Inn and usually a bottle of something more stimulating that well-water, although I am sure that Molly consumed more of each than her recumbent guest.

The visits followed a similar pattern. I would arrive with my basket and a ready, if forced, smile and ask: 'how is he today?'

Molly would take and empty the basket, reply, 'much the same as yesterday' and bring me upstairs to view my Frenchman. There followed the most interesting part of the day as I removed Merlin the cat from his nest of blankets and carefully shaved my Frenchman. After that I would sit at the side of his bed and talk to him in English, which he would neither hear nor understand, while watching his now familiar monkey-face. There were occasions when I nicked his skin while shaving him so that necessitated finding a towel and cleaning up the blood. I never inflicted a serious wound, I am glad to say.

After a while Molly would wander up the stairs. 'Are you going to spend all day with that silent man?'

'Not all day,' I said, although in truth there was something quite relaxing about talking to a man who did not speak back or try to sort out problems I was not aware that I had.

After that I would tell Molly's the day's news and she would tell me hers, mostly about her hens not laying or her goats milking. Occasionally she would have a more interesting tit-bit, such as the day she told me she saw Kitty and her new sweetheart skipping hand in hand to the old lighthouse or chantry or whatever people now term the structure is that stands erect on St Catherine's Down.

'Oh tell me more,' I insisted and listened avidly as Molly described exactly what Kitty and her beau had been up to, with great anatomical detail that would have shocked a marine and had me in stitches of laughter and some hidden jealousy as well, for so far in my life I had never experienced such pleasures. Now don't forget these jealousies because they had a part to play in my decision with the gallant captain. A girl has certain needs you know, and in my line of work I witnessed a constant flow of men and women through their lives of meeting, marrying and bearing children; I felt quite neglected at times with my poor Lieutenant Baldivere lying cold in his grave and me lying equally chill in my lonely bed.

There were other tit-bits that turned me a lesser shade of green, and some that stilled the blood in my veins.

'The Volunteers were searching again,' Molly spoke almost casually. 'They knocked on every door in the parish asking if anybody had heard anything of a fugitive smuggler.'

I could not help my furtive glance upstairs where my Frenchman was lying alone. 'Did you tell them anything?'

'Of course not,' Molly said. She was silent for a few moments. 'I don't think he can stay here for ever though. Once the Volunteers get bored with merely asking, they will start searching the houses and I can't hide a hulking great man like that inside my clothes chest.'

'I'll think of something,' I said, although in truth I had no idea at all what to do with him. Wight is not a huge island and if the Volunteers, or worse the regular redcoats decided to rummage through every house and cottage there were few places where I could hide him. The only alternative I could think of was Limestone Manor, which had been empty for so long that nobody would ever look there; unless Mr Howard and his French friends had another meeting there, of course. Honestly, whoever said 'what a tangled web we weave, when first we practise to deceive' knew what he was talking about. It must have been a man who wrote that because women don't have to admit such things.

After that little conversation it was time for me to have a last look at Monkey-face with the slightly razor-nicked face and the healing bruise on his forehead, and return back to the Inn. These meetings became a fixed routine for some time, until my Frenchmen woke again.

As luck would have it, I was shaving him at the time. I had lathered his face and was stroking the open razor down his left cheek when his eyes popped open and I found myself staring into them. They were of the deepest green, like a winter sea, and looked utterly startled to see me.

He said something in French.

'Hello,' I responded. 'I am afraid I can't understand a word you are saying.'

He spoke again, trying to sit up and putting a hand on my arm, as if to prevent me shaving him. After all it must be quite disconcerting to wake up and have some stray foreign woman flashing a great sharp blade an inch or two from one's throat.

'It's all right,' I said, holding up the razor so he could see it better. 'I am just trying to shave you.' I made gestures with the razor across my own face to reassure him. I am not sure if he smiled or not as I resumed shaving operations on his face, moving my hand very gently in case he should suddenly sit up, or launch into singing *La Marseillaise* or try to conquer the island or maybe leap out the window and make a dash for freedom.

I could feel his eyes on me, watching everything I was doing. I tried to relax him by speaking as I worked, 'there we are, removing all that ugly stubble; nice and smooth now; around your lips next and what lovely lips they are too, some lady will enjoy kissing them; do you have a sweetheart? I wager you do; I wager you have a whole host of sweethearts back in France all desperate to kiss these lips of yours. They will be missing you now, lost in England and cared for by Molly and me.'

'I have no sweetheart.' My Frenchman said in the most delightful accent I had ever heard.

'No?' I looked at him in astonishment. 'You are awake then; and speaking in English again.'

He looked at me and slowly, gently smiled.

I thought it best to encourage him to speak more. 'Do the women in France not like handsome men?' I had heard so many rumours about Frenchwomen that I did not know what to believe.

My Frenchman looked blank. 'I don't remember,' he said. 'You are very kind taking care of me.'

That stopped me. I had been called many things in my life but kind was not one of them. 'I am not kind in the slightest,' I told him.

'I think you are,' my Frenchman said.

'Well, I said, rudely, for I was angrier than I should have been, but I was young enough to wish certain perceptions thought about me. 'You know what thought did, don't you?'

'No,' he said, 'I don't know.'

'Thought stuck his bottom out the window and ran outside because he *thought* he could throw stones at it!' I was so cross with this man for thinking me kind that I grew careless with the razor and nicked his chin. A ruby drop of blood formed amidst the frothy soap and smeared the blade of my razor. 'Oh God, I'm sorry!' I said, immediately contrite.

He had not flinched. 'I won't be throwing stones at myself,' he said. His eyes had not left my face. 'What's your name?'

'I am Sarah,' I said. 'Sarah Bembridge.' I carried on with the shaving, taking more care.

'Sarah.' My Frenchman rolled the syllables around his tongue. 'That is a nice name. Soft, easy on the mouth.'

'Easier than my shaving anyway,' I said. 'And what's your name anyway. It is Pierre? Or Marcel? Isn't that what all Frenchmen are called?'

'Oh no, I'm Charles; Charles Louis Durand.' He said the name so naturally that I thought he had fully recovered.

'Well Charles,' I wiped the last of the soap from his face and stepped back, 'it is good to finally know your name.' I gave a little curtsey and held out my hand in a formal greeting.

His smile was small but welcome as he took my hand. I was prepared for him to kiss it, in the French manner, but instead he gave it an honest shake and returned it to me unsullied and unkissed. I felt a trifle disappointed. Perhaps the Republican French did not approve of hand-kissing, I thought, which seemed a little strange of them.

'Welcome to Wight,' I said.

'Thank you,' Charles looked confused. 'How did I get here?'

'You were on a French ship,' I told him, 'and you either fell overboard or were blown overboard by a cannon and were washed up on the shore here.'

Charles shook his head. 'Why was I on a French ship? I can't remember anything about it.'

I smiled. 'You were on a French ship because you are French,' I said. 'You do speak English very well for a Frenchman.'

Charles looked down at himself. 'Where am I? Where are my clothes? When can I go home?'

I laughed out loud, 'so many questions from one man and all at the same time!' It was good to have Charles talking after so long, yet I really hoped he might know more about himself. It seemed that he had lost some of his memory when he had fallen in the sea.

'What's all the noise about?' Molly poked her head through the door. 'Oh so we're awake are we?'

'His name is Charles Louis Durand and he does not remember anything about anything,' I said. 'Charles, say good afternoon to Molly Draper, your host here.'

'Good afternoon,' Charles said politely. He looked at me. 'I thought you were my host.'

'I am only a visitor. Molly here is the host.'

Somehow Charles managed to bow from his position lying in bed. 'Thank you for your hospitality, Mrs Draper.'

Molly nodded. 'It is Miss Draper,' she said. 'And there are men looking for you.'

Charles smiled, 'maybe they can tell me more about myself?'

'Or maybe they will shoot you,' Molly said. 'We can't allow them to find you.'

I met Charles' gaze. I had grown to rather like this monkey-faced man who had lain so quiet. Now I liked his interesting French accent. I did not want to see him shot by some over-zealous Volunteer, or locked in the Hulks or whatever hell-hole the government incarcerated their French prisoners.

I resolved to find some more secure accommodation for my smiling French-man and if that meant I was committing treason against the Crown, well, the Crown had never bowed to me from a bed, or smiled when I nicked its chin with an open razor. Nor was it particularly handsome, in a monkey-faced, inquisitive sort of way. You will notice that I had quite forgiven Charles for calling me kind, although I knew I had a lot of work ahead of me.

Chapter Fifteen

So you see, when Captain Chadwick asked me to marry him, my mind was quite busy with things other than matrimony. I had Kitty's flirting to think about and my poor Charles to move somewhere safer than Molly's house, as well as my own work in the Inn and David's sad demise.

I must have stared at Captain Chadwick with my mouth open for a good half-minute before I could even think of a reply.

'Why Captain Chadwick,' I eventually managed to stutter. 'I am over-whelmed. I had no idea that you felt that way about me.' Well I had an inkling I suppose but I did not take his attentions as seriously as I might.

Captain Chadwick smiled. 'Oh my dear,' he said, taking one of my hands in his. 'I have been so concerned about you ever since Lieutenant … David … your poor husband … died. You were so forlorn.'

'Oh,' I looked to Mother, who raised her eyebrows and said nothing, leaving me alone in that room full of people. I honestly did not know what to do and what to say. 'I have to think,' I said.

'Of course you do,' Captain Chadwick said. 'I do not expect an instant reply.'

He did not get one. I ran from the tap-room and up to the fresh air of the Downs. I am not sure how I got there, but I found myself at the Long Stone, that most ancient of monuments on Wight where I had wooed poor David, and I sat on the ground with my arms around my knees and my head even more of a whirl than it normally was.

Now, you may think me foolish to act so. I know that any girl in my position should have leaped at the chance to marry such a man as Captain Chadwick. If you compare our positions, you will see why.

I was the daughter of an inn-keeper with no money, no education and no prospects.

He was a captain of Volunteers, holding the King's commission and doubtless with some sort of property and wealth behind him.

I was twenty years old and already a widow. If I did manage to find a local husband he would be a fisherman or a skipper at best. If I did not, I was destined to work for my bed-and-board in the inn until my mother died in twenty, thirty or forty years, by which time I would be old, worn-out, grey and useless.

So you see, I had little choice in the matter. You can also see that the romantic idealism with which I viewed my liaison to David was gone. I did not have any such rosy-hued notions about Captain Chadwick; he was much older than me and I had no illusions about mutual love. I wanted security in my life and he, whatever his claims about concern for me after David's death, wanted a young wife to bounce in bed and show off in the streets of Dublin or wherever he happened to be posted.

Well, I had no qualms about being shown off and I could cope with the bed-room antics as long as he was not too old for me. It was then that I remembered Kitty and her sweetheart at the old lighthouse. I recalled my jealousy at her romping while I was left with the frustrated memories of a man whose sole attempt to seduce me had been clumsy and unwelcome at best. I was twenty, remember, and a normal healthy woman with a normal healthy appetite. Maybe Kitty had a younger man, but I had one with substance and position. I would be a captain's wife, one of the most high-ranking women in the regiment and all those self- important women who had turned up their noses at me at my last wedding had better learn manners before my next or I would use my new rank to make their lives as unpleasant as possible.

I grinned at that thought, leaning back against the warm standing stone. At the time of my first wedding I had tried to disregard the attitude of those women. Now I was determined to make them pay for their long noses and frosty demeanours. As the captain's wife I would outrank them as surely as Captain Chadwick outranked their husbands. Oh I would make them dance attendance on me!

I tossed my hair at that thought and stretched, looking out to sea where there were the usual quota of sails and a pestilential revenue cutter nosing around just offshore. With that cutter so busy, our free traders would find it hard to bring their cargoes in and Mother's profits would fall. French brandy was a favourite among all the Overners who dropped in, particularly the soldiers and naval officers and Mother always bumped the price up for their benefit.

I stood up and embraced the Long Stone. It had stood me in good stead again, helping to order my thoughts and make a decision. Now I had to find out all I could about Captain Chadwick so I could be a loving and dutiful wife to him, as long as he was a considerate and faithful husband to me, of course. If Kitty could cuddle up to some handsome man, then so could I.

The path back to the Horse Head seemed lighter than that I had traversed on my outward journey. I nearly sang as I walked, nodding to a number of farm servants as they wound their weary way homeward, and I even admired the fields of grain. This war may have been a bit of a nuisance with all the alarums and scarums, but without it Wight would not have been half so prosperous. Most of the local proprietors including Hugo Bertram had increased their acreage of wheat to sell to the navy and Bertram had even built his own mill to make flour. Only the lands of Limestone Manor were neglected: that place was a horrible blight on the landscape. Thinking of Limestone Manor reminded me of Charles and how I had to create a place to hide him in case my latest husband-to-be decided to become more efficient in his search for the supposed smuggler.

I thought then that one did not have total loyalty to one's husband. He was only one factor in life, as I would be only one factor in his. Satisfied with my new standpoint that was so different to my feelings for poor David, I walked into the Horse Head.

Chapter Sixteen

Mother looked up as soon as I entered. I think she had some sort of power that helped her to know when her daughter was around.

'Well Sarah,' she said quietly, 'have you had time to think?' She did not comment on the tear stains that must have been obvious on my face.

'I have,' I said, 'and my answer will be yes.'

Mother nodded. 'Captain Chadwick will be pleased,' she did not that if she was pleased or not. 'Have you had sufficient time? You do not have to give your answer right away.' She stepped closer to me and lowered her voice. 'Don't say yes if you are unsure.'

'I have thought about that,' I said, 'and I think the advantages outweigh any disadvantages. He and I will have to discuss the details first and then we will discuss and set the date and location, which will be the chapel at Knighton Hazard.'

Mother's smile was rueful. 'He may not agree to that.'

'In that he has no choice,' I said. 'You have always said I am a stubborn hussie and a stubborn hussie I will remain.'

Mother laughed at that, although her eyes were not as happy as I would have preferred. 'I fear that poor Captain Chadwick may not have the dutiful and obedient wife he may wish for.' For a reason I did not then understand, she looked quite relieved at the thought.

Mr Howard was not at the Horse Head at the time. He came in later and once I had attended to Chocolate he ordered his supper and retired to a corner table in the tap-room, from where he surveyed our customers without speaking to anybody.

'Are you all right, Mr Howard?' I asked him. 'You look very worried these past few days.' I did not add that his French friends had been notable by their absence. One does not rub salt into the wound of a paying guest, whatever his political sympathies.

Mr Howard looked up. I swear he had aged since he arrived at our inn. There were deeper grooves running from the corners of his mouth to his nose and I was adamant that his hair was a touch more grey. 'I am not sure that my mission here will be a success,' he said frankly, 'and that grieves me greatly.'

I did not say that I knew what his mission was and could not share in his hopes. Although I felt sympathy with him as a man, I had no desire to have French soldiers tramping all over my island. It was bad enough with the redcoat regulars and the Volunteers. Except for Captain Chadwick of course, who was the finest gentleman ever to don the King's uniform.

Even as I thought the name, the good Captain walked into the inn.

'Please excuse me,' I gave Mr Howard my second best curtsey and fled toward my future husband.

'Ah, Miss Bembridge,' Captain Chadwick greeted me. 'Have you made your decision yet? There is no rush, but it would be good to have all the arrangements made before the regiment sails for Dublin.'

I took a deep breath. 'Captain Chadwick,' I said, 'are you certain that you wish to spend the remainder of your life with me? I am only an inn-keeper's daughter...' I had to stop then as he put his finger against my lips.

'If I was not certain,' he said, 'I would not have asked.'

'In that case, sir,' I gave my best ever curtsey, which meant my skirt helped brush the floor while my head was roughly level with Captain Chadwick's belt buckle, 'I would be honoured to accept.'

Captain Chadwick's smile was sufficiently broad to be seen from France, yet alone in that smokey tap-room. 'The honour, my dear Miss Bembridge, is all mine.' He stepped into the centre of the room and raised his voice to a parade-ground roar. 'I wish to announce that Miss Bembridge has this moment consented to become my wife. In honour of the occasion I will buy drinks for everybody in this august establishment for the next hour.'

Apart from one silly old josser commenting that it was June, not August, my dear Captain Chadwick's offer met with a spontaneous rush to the counter before he changed his mind. Such is the way of the world that free drink was more the topic of conversation than my impending wedding.

'The happy couple!' My mother raised a glass to toast us, although I noted that she did not offer to pay for the brandy she pretended to down before pouring it back into a jug. Some unsuspecting customer would drink that later, so doubling Mother's profits for brandy she probably bought for a song in the first place. Honestly, they say that the French War increased the National Debt. If they had put my mother in charge of the Treasury Great Britain would have come out of the war with a healthy surplus, even if all the inhabitants of the country were permanently inebriated.

'We will get married in Knighton Hazard,' I said that loudly so there was no room for doubt. 'It is a habit I have.'

My humour was not lost on Captain Chadwick, whose laugh echoed around the tap-room. The only person who did not join in the laughter was Mr Howard, who sat in his corner seat and watched me through quiet, brooding eyes.

Chapter Seventeen

I was always aware that Mr Howard was constantly watching me. He had been doing so since the first day that he had arrived. His eyes were friendly, musing, sometimes even amused, yet still quite disturbing as they followed my every movement around the tap-room and in the stables.

I wondered if he knew that I had seen him in Limestone Manor. If so, he kept very quiet about it, as did I.

Every morning Mr Howard would leave the inn on horseback and most nights he would return late. When I tended to Chocolate I often noticed his legs spattered with mud. They were particularly filthy the day following my engagement to Captain Chadwick.

'You are riding Chocolate hard, sir' I said, rubbing her fetlocks.

'I can do that when it is needed,' he said.

'Mr Howard,' I tried to forget that he was a Frenchman. 'May I be able to help you in your quest? I have noticed you riding all over Wight, day after day, and occasionally visiting Limestone Manor that you asked about.'

'I am searching for somebody,' Mr Howard said.

'You have been more than kind to me since David's death,' I was learning to be as blunt as Mother when the time was right, yet I could smooth my words with sugar when it would help. 'I know most everybody in this part of the island and can find out about the rest. If you tell me for whom you seek I can try and help.' I still do not know how genuine my offer was. My loyalties were torn you see, between my patriotism to Great Britain and my growing realisation that people who cared for me mattered every bit as much as some ethereal feeling for king and country. Yet I did not want Boney's armies marching across Wight.

'The person I am searching for is not a local,' Mr Howard said. 'I am not even sure that he is alive.'

'Does he have a name?'

'Charles Louis Durand,' Mr Howard told me immediately, with no expression. He said the name as the French pronounced it, as Charles had pronounced it himself.

'That is a French name,' I spoke without thought to hide the sudden turmoil within me.

'It is a French name,' Mr Howard did not drop his gaze.

I decided to press a little harder. 'Is that the same man that the Volunteers are searching for?'

'That's the man,' Mr Howard said quietly.

'You are not in the army,' I said. 'Are you an Exciseman?' I was being as blunt as my mother; perhaps that was my new maturity as the pending wife of a captain of Volunteers.

'I am not an Exciseman,' Mr Howard said.

I did not ask what he was. I told him instead. 'You are some sort of official,' I said. I did not say that I knew he was an official of the French. I did not want him to know that I knew. Perhaps Mr Howard, as he called himself, was keeping his eyes on me, but I was also keeping a watch on him in my own way. Once I was married to Captain Chadwick I would tell my husband and he would have this enigmatic, quiet-eyed and probably very dangerous man arrested, although I certainly did not want him executed. If I had, I would have reported him many days ago. As the wife of Captain Chadwick, I hoped I would have sufficient influence to save his life.

Mr Howard nodded. 'I am as you say,' he agreed. 'I am some sort of official.' His eyes never strayed from mine. 'If you do hear anything of Charles Durand,' he said, 'or if you hear any rumours or tales of a stranger hiding on the island, could you please let me know? It is very important to me.'

I nodded. 'I will tell you,' I said. I think that was the only lie I have ever told in my life and I hated to say it. Poor Mr Howard looked so worried and forlorn that I desperately wanted to help him. If it had been anybody else but Charles, I may well have told him everything, even if that meant breaking one of the cardinal codes of the Chalkheads: what happens in the Back of Wight stays in the Back of Wight.

'Thank you,' Mr Howard reached out and squeezed my hand. 'You are a good girl, Sarah, a good, kind girl.'

At that moment I hated myself more than I had ever done before.

Chapter Eighteen

'So this is your special place?' Captain Chadwick stood in the shadow of the Long Stone and admired the view. I stood a few paces away and admired Captain Chadwick.

'This is where I come when I have to think things out, and where I come with special people.'

He was certainly older than David. 'How old are you, Captain Chadwick?'

'I am thirty-three next summer.' Captain Chadwick was taller than my last husband as well, and perhaps an inch or two broader. Really he was a most distinguished looking man. I allowed my eyes to roam down his body, so trim within his tight scarlet tunic.

'No,' Captain Chadwick must have read my thoughts. 'I do not wear a stomacher or anything else to keep my shape.' He looked at me with a smile. 'I am as fit now as I was when I was your age.'

'Thank you, Captain,' I said.

'Did you bring Lieutenant – did you bring David here?' Captain Chadwick asked.

I nodded, trying not to make comparisons.

Captain Chadwick put his hand on my shoulder. 'This might help you forget,' he said, and kissed me. It was not the most passionate of kisses; rather it was soft and gentle, a kiss by a man who was used to kissing; a man's kiss rather than a kiss by an eager boy.

I felt myself respond, opening my mouth beneath him and gasping as his tongue flickered into my own.

'Why Captain Chadwick,' I said, more in surprise than shock.

'That is rather formal, don't you think?' Captain Chadwick said. 'Would William not be better between husband and wife?'

'We are not husband and wife yet,' I reminded, for in truth I was rather concerned that this wedding would not come about. I still believed that no captain of Volunteers would see anything advantageous in marrying an inn-keeper's daughter. Our social differences were quite extreme.

'In all but name,' William said with the most amiable of smiles. 'And I should call you Sarah, if you would permit me?'

'I would much prefer that to Miss Bembridge,' I said. 'It feels much more comfortable.' And more secure, I thought. No stranger would call a lady by her Christian name. It was a small step toward our ultimate objective. To be a captain's wife! That was far beyond my greatest dreams.

William stepped back once more and surveyed the landscape. He pointed to the great ruined tower that Hugo Bertram was in the process of building at the highest height of his policies. The ugly structure overlooked the chapel and house of Knighton Hazard. 'What on earth is Hugo creating there?'

I noted he and Mr Bertram were on first name terms. 'It is a folly,' I said. I did not wish to say more than that.

'I see,' William said. 'Is there a point to it? Is he going to stand on top and watch for the French, perhaps? Or maybe use a horn to call in his cattle?'

'No,' I said. 'It is rather a sad story. Mr Bertram is building it as a celebration that his wife left him. They did not have the happiest of marriages.'

William's laughter was possibly out of place yet better than most reactions. 'Well, my sweet Sarah,' he said, 'we must make sure that we have no need to build such a folly.'

'Indeed not, William,' I said, and linked my arm with his. At times like these it was good to know that one's husband-to-be had a sense of humour and did not take other people's misfortunes as a sign of his own future.

He hugged me close and released me, waving his hand around the Back of Wight that was spread out before us.

'We believe there is a Frenchman hiding somewhere out there,' he said. 'I do hope we can catch him before the regiment is sent to Dublin. It would be a feather in our caps and a blow, albeit a minor one, to Bonaparte.' He looked at me and placed his hand on my shoulder in gentlemanly, husbandly concern. 'I am worried when you walk alone in the island with that ruffian on the loose, you see.'

'Oh,' I said for I was touched by his genuine concern. For a moment I even contemplated telling him about Charles and getting this thing all cleared up. No, I thought; wait until we are married and I know him better. A man may listen and take heed of his wife's advice when he will only seek to impress his sweetheart, affianced or not.

'I will be all right,' I said. 'I know many people in Wight and we look after our own here.' I ran my hands over the Long Stone. 'This is my island you see; and this is my stone; where I belong.'

'You will soon belong to the Regiment, as I do.' William told me. 'We may return to the island sometime, when this war is over and Bonaparte lies in his grave.'

That sobered me I can tell you. The thought of travelling to Dublin or some such exotic place was exciting, yet I had not truly contemplated the other side of that spinning coin. I had only ever known Wight; it was where I belonged and I did not know how I would survive without Mother and Molly and Captain Nash, Buckett and my Long Stone. Even Kitty, with her foibles and man-hunger, my dearest friend that I loved to hate to distraction, emulate and scorn, was as close to me as any sister. How could I live happily when I was parted from them? I wondered what dear Kitty was doing at that moment, what poor un-suspecting boy she was seducing, and what tales she would have to tell when next I saw her.

'Oh come, come.' Even though he was a man, William had noticed my change of mood and, surprisingly, had guessed the reason. 'I will bring you back as of-ten as convenient, my dear Sarah. Why, once you have seen Dublin and London or even Edinburgh, Athens of the North or perhaps France when we occupy that country, you may not wish to return to this green little island.'

Suddenly I did not wish to travel to Dublin or London, the northern Athens or France. I wished to remain in my own, my very own, green little island where everything was that I held dear. I am sure that tears formed in my eye as I thought of leaving, until Captain Chadwick cheered me with another kiss and a pat on my shoulder.

'Don't take on so, old girl,' he said. 'Come, come, this is a happy time. See what I have brought for you.' Reaching into an inside pocket, he produced a small box.

Now, I have never been a woman for feminine knick-knacks. Perhaps because I have never owned any or even dreamed of owning such trivia, yet when William pulled out that small red box I was instantly intrigued.

'What can it be?' I wondered as he held it out a hand's-breadth from my nose, pulling it away as I reached for it.

'Oh don't tease me so,' I pleaded as William stepped back, smiling as he held the box just out of my grasp.

'Is this for you? Or shall I replace it where I found it,' William said, walking backward around the Long Stone as I followed him with small steps and rising anticipation.

'It's for me,' I said, hearing the nearly childish giggle in my voice. Honestly I have not acted so since I was about eight years old but William had such a way about him that I could not help myself. Besides, the contents of that box intrigued me beyond endurance.

'Oh all right, then,' William stopped and lowered his hand. I took the box gingerly, half expecting some trick. 'Open it then.'

I did. Inside, sitting on a bed of crumpled red silk, was the most beautiful ring that anybody could have dreamed of. Set on a shaft of gold, a single diamond was surrounded by nine red rubies, each one sparkling in the sun.

'It's perfect,' I said, staring at this wondrous creation.

'Rings generally look better when they are on a finger,' William told me. 'Here, allow me.' Removing the ring from its box, he took my left hand and with the utmost gentleness he slipped it onto the finger next to my pinkie. It was very slightly loose but not enough to cause me any worries about losing it. Instead it sat there, snug as if it had been made for me and sparkling like the pride of an Empress.

I stared at it. 'Is that for me?' I asked. I had never worn jewellery of any sort before, yet alone something that must have cost a queen's ransom. 'I can't imagine wearing this as I clean out the stables,' I said, and laughed.

'That's just it, Sarah,' William said quietly. 'When you are my wife, you won't ever need to clean out stables again, or do any more of these menial tasks. We will have servants for such things. You will be mistress of our household, giving orders and having others run about at your bidding.'

I stared at the ring again. Although I heard what William said I am not sure if I quite understood the full implications of my forthcoming marriage. The social leap between skivvy at an inn and wife of a captain of Volunteers was something I had not properly comprehended. 'Oh William,' I said and repeated myself. 'Oh William.'

'Does that make you feel better about leaving this island of yours?' William asked.

'Oh yes,' I replied at once.

'And does it deserve just a little kiss?'

'Oh yes indeed,' I said, hardly able to take my gaze from the ring as he put two gentle hands on my face.

I kissed him again, then, tenderly at first and then will increasing passion as we pressed closer to each other. A kiss is an amazing thing you know. It is so simple in itself and yet it can unleash such a torrent of diverse emotions from satisfaction to reassurance and even the wildest of desires.

However I had no deep desires, no passion for more intimacy when I kissed William, although I did feel his body react against mine. I smiled at that; it is a good feeling to know that one has the ability to arouse a man to passion, especially when that man is to be one's husband. For a second I thought of Kitty and how often she gloated over her undoubted power with men. She would be wild with jealousy the second she saw my ring.

I pulled back to view my ring again. *My* ring. I could have looked at it for hours if only to catch the glitter of the sun on the stones and the way the light reflected from each sharp edge. However I had things to do.

'One last kiss,' I said, breathlessly, 'and then I must be off. I have my work to do for Mother and I have to show off my new ring. Have you seen it?' I held it up so the sun could catch the circle of rubies.

'I have,' William said. 'It is a fine ring.'

We kissed once more, passionately, with William's hands wandering where they would on my back and flanks and even, daringly, further south than any gentleman should venture unless to his wedded wife. I allowed that, though, as he had presented me with such a fine ring, and I even pressed against him, momentarily, to allow him a small taste of the delights to come. 'Once we are married,' I said, with a small smile, 'we will have such fun.'

'Yes indeed,' William sounded somewhat breathless as I broke free, glanced again at my new ring, gave him a final peck on the cheek, turned and fled across the downs, thinking how green with envy Kitty would be. I had never owned such a fine ring and at that second I knew that neither had anybody else.

Captain Chadwick must truly love me to purchase such a magnificent ring just for me.

Chapter Nineteen

Yet strangely, it was not to Kitty that I ran, nor even to Mother, but to Molly's secluded cottage with her friendly goats and the buzz of honey-bees in the row of hives outside.

'What do you think about that?' I asked Charles as he lay in his bed with Merlin curled up at his side. 'It is a ring from my intended.'

'You are to be married?' To my disappointment Charles barely glanced at the ring. Perhaps men have less interest in such things as we do. Instead he looked directly into my face. 'To whom?'

For a Frenchman his language really was impressive. 'To Captain William Chadwick,' I told him. 'The commander of the St Catherine's Volunteers.'

Charles' smile was forced. As I knew he liked me and so would be happy for me I thought his discomposure must arise from constipation and decided to ask Molly for a tonic for him. One must ensure that one's bowels are kept mobile, you know, as Mother continually harped on to me. A concoction of Aloa Vera, dandelions, nettles and sena should do the trick. I vowed to check on my patient later, quite proud that I had heeded some of my mother's teachings, if disappointed that Charles' reaction to my ring was not quite all that I hoped for.

I heard Molly banging her feet quite hard on the stairs before she stepped in. 'How are you both today?' She had been milking the goats and handed over a stoneware mug to Charles. 'You drink this.' She listened to my diagnosis of his disposition and nodded.

'That would help,' she said, 'unless there is another reason for his reaction.' She did not explain further. 'Do you have a sore finger?'

'Why, no,' I said in surprise.

'You seem to have some sort of growth on it,' Molly pointed to my ring.

'William gave me that,' I said and enjoyed her admiration. Honestly, women are so much more appreciative than men about the important things in life.

'It is the most splendid ring,' Molly said, twisting it, and my finger, this way and that until I nearly had to cry for her to desist. 'I am sure Captain William must have travelled miles to find such a thing. I cannot conceive of a jeweller's shop in all of Wight where he could find it.'

'He must have sailed to the mainland,' I said.

'Perhaps that is what he did,' Molly said.

'That is a sure sign of true love,' I knew I sounded smug but I cared not a whit. Molly glanced at Charles and pulled a face.

'That reminds me,' I said, 'there is a man in the Horse Head who knows your name, Charles, and he is searching for you.'

Charles half rose. 'He cannot know me,' he said, 'for I scarce know myself. What is this fellow's name?'

'He calls himself Mr Adam Howard,' I said, 'and I believe he may be as French as you are although he also speaks the most perfect English.'

Charles pulled a most amusing face. 'Mr Howard. I do not remember that name.'

'He has a horse called Chocolate,' I added, 'if that helps. He has spent an amazing amount of time riding about the island in pursuit of you.' Now I had started I thought it best to tell all.

Molly held my hand as I related my tale about Mr Howard and the Frenchmen at Limestone Manor, while Charles looked worried, as he had every cause to.

'It's all right,' I reassured him, 'we will keep you safe.'

'More importantly,' he said, 'is that you both keep yourselves safe. These are dangerous times.' He blinked. 'Good Lord... I remember something!'

'What?' I knelt on the bed in my excitement, nearly crushing the poor man's legs as I thumped down on top of him. Merlin howled in protest at this unwarranted intrusion on what he now regarded as his own territory.

'I remembered a face,' Charles said.

'What face? Was it Mr Howard? What did he look like?' I was full of questions.

'It was a woman,' Charles said. I did not expect the sudden stab of pain that hit me, or the surge of anger that nearly had me slapping my poor French castaway. 'A most beautiful woman.'

'Was it indeed,' I heard the coldness of my tone as I resolved to rid myself of the burden of this intolerable Frenchman as soon as possible. Why was I even bothering about him? I should have reported him as soon as I knew he was French. Here was I, soon to be the wife of a commissioned officer in the Volunteers and I was pandering to the whims of a damned French Republican who had probably killed a score of honest Britons on his privateering missions. Why, he might even have been responsible for the death of my father, damn his eyes and soul for causing me pain.

Pain? How could some stray French before-the-mast seaman possibly cause me pain? What nonsense.

I forced a smile. 'Could it be your sweetheart perhaps? Or even your wife?'

'No, I don't believe so,' this disturbing, monkey-faced man said. 'She was too old for that.'

'Your mother, then?' Molly had noticed my reaction and strove to pour soothing oil over my troubled waters.

'Yes!' Dear, sweet Charles nearly bounded out of the bed in his delight. 'She must have been my mother!'

My forgiveness was instant of course, and total. 'What was she like? Do you know from where she came? If we know what port you come from, I am sure that Captain Buckett could arrange some sort of meeting with a French fisherman that would see you sent home; if that is what you wish.'

Suddenly I had no desire to see the back of my addle-headed Frenchman. We had all heard of the horrors of Republican France where the guillotine awaited any who did not obey their obnoxious new laws and where conscription into the ever-hungry army waited every male from teenage boys to even quite elderly men. France was an armed camp and Bonaparte clung to power by declaring endless war on every nation in Europe and by having an army of spies and agents reporting on all his citizens.

Agents such as Mr Howard?

'I wish I could remember,' Charles said. He coloured a second later. 'Not that I wish to say farewell to you two ladies. You have been better than welcoming and I am deeply grateful for your kindness.' He took my right hand in his right, and Molly's in his left. 'I wish there was some way in which I could thank you. If ever I remember who I am or from where I come, I will do all I can to repay you.'

'I could ask Mr Howard who you are,' I said. 'When I last tried he shut his mouth as tight as a mussel. I can try again.'

'Please do,' Charles said. 'It is most irritating not knowing who I am or from where I come.'

'The Volunteers are also looking for you,' I said. 'I think we had best find somewhere safer for you.'

'Where?' Molly asked.

'Limestone Manor,' I told her. 'Hardly anybody ever goes there; there is plenty space and I am sure we can find a suitable room.' The decision was made. The decision that nearly cost us all our lives.

Chapter Twenty

There were more guests at my second wedding than there had been at my first. On one side of the square room were the Caulkheads, smiling and chatting together like the old friends that they were. Unfortunately there were a few notable absentees, with Captain Nash and James Buckett out at sea and Mr Howard away on one of his usual mysterious absences. I was glad to see that both Molly and Kitty were there, the former sitting stiff in clothes far more formal than was her wont and the latter fluttering her eyelashes at every male in scarlet, while running a critical gaze over the dress, looks and attitude of every one of their wives. I also saw her making sheep's eyes at my William and hoped she enjoyed the privilege, the green-eyed minx.

Talking of Volunteers, all the officers were present, and all their wives, making a phalanx of scarlet interspersed with a rainbow of bright colours on one side of the chapel at Knighton Hazard. Officers from other regiments were also present to see Captain Chadwick married off, and even some of the great and good of the island.

'You are indeed in exalted company,' Mother said as she made minute and unnecessary adjustments to my wedding dress, patted my hair into place and plumped my bonnet on top as if I were a child going to Sunday School. 'There now,' she stepped back to inspect me, 'you look good enough to eat.' She gave me a very unusual hug, patted my shoulder and kissed me on the nose. 'Please try and keep this husband a little longer than you kept the last. I would dearly like some grandchildren to help run the inn.'

'Yes, Mother,' I said dutifully. 'I hope you have remembered that William and I are off to Dublin next month.'

'Oh so you are; that quite slipped my memory,' Mother said. I knew that was an untruth. She had been secretly packing a trunk for me these past two weeks. I had also heard her cry into her pillow at night, although when I challenged her over it she had stoutly denied doing any such thing.

Now I stood just outside the chapel, looking in. I was more nervous than last time, possibly because my next husband was over ten years older than me and of a much higher social standing, or perhaps because of the impending move to Dublin, away from everything and everybody I had ever known.

The Reverend Barwis smiled as he saw me. 'The best of luck,' he whispered and continued with the ceremony. I only heard half of it as I thought of the future life I would have, occasionally swivelling my eyes to look at this tall man who was to be my constant companion for many years to come, and perhaps even the father of my children. He was in his best uniform with the scarlet bright in the chapel and the gold braid gleaming under the crystal chandelier. I had never seen him smarter or more handsome, and I felt my breath stop within my throat that this handsome, elegant man was very soon to be my husband.

The service droned on with my excitement mounting as I neared the actual declaration when I should say 'I do' and commit myself. There was one interesting moment when the Reverend Barwis asked if anybody knew of anybody who might object and Molly chose that moment to burst into a fit of coughing. I turned around and glared at her.

'My apologies, Sarah,' Molly said in a loud, clear voice. 'I don't know what came over me.' And then she gave me a huge wink that nearly set me giggling in front of the Reverend Barwis, my nearly-husband and the entire congregation.

However, once that little incident was over the remainder of the ceremony proceeded without a hitch and we were proclaimed as husband and wife. Once again the Reverend Barwis invited my new husband to kiss me and once again he did so, to the restrained applause of the crowd. It was not much of a kiss, really, more like a brief peck. I expected more later, and I intended to get it too.

I was pleased when we escaped from that chapel with the two portraits of Mr and Mrs Ebenezer Bertram looking down upon us from either side of the door and the memories of poor David's unfortunate demise in my head. I had hoped to have the wedding breakfast in the Horse Head but William had insisted that it should be elsewhere. I think he believed our inn was not grand enough for either of us. So instead we happily repaired the short distance to Knighton Hazard, where Hugo Bertram had invited we share his hospitality.

That was a very happy walk across a trim lawn with hardly a buttercup or daisy in view and bird-song the best music in my world.

I had no hand in the arrangements so was acutely astonished when I walked in to see the entire great hall of Knighton Hazard set up with long tables that groaned under the weight of food and green branches arrayed above. In the centre of the top table was the largest cake that I had ever seen in my life. One layer piled above another, it was beautifully iced and topped with two small wooden figures of a man and woman that must have taken some craftsman hours to carve and an artist patient skill to paint.

'I have never seen anything so beautiful,' I said.

William laughed. 'Well, Sarah, you can get used to such things. I have heard that Dublin is one of the most elegant cities in the land.'

For the first time in my life I also had a dozen servants to wait upon my husband and I – and all the other guests I suppose – and Hugo was the first to approach me.

'Mrs Chadwick!' he said loudly, whereupon I looked around the room, thinking that my esteemed mother-in-law had decided to pay us a surprise visit. It took me a few moments to realise that I was now Mrs Chadwick and put my hand to my mouth in surprise.

'May I congratulate you on your new name,' Hugo said with a deep bow.

'Thank you, Mr Bertram,' I said, dropping my hand so he could hear m.

'Hugo,' he said softly. 'You must call me Hugo now, and I call you Sarah, or Mrs Chadwick if you prefer.'

'Oh!' I put my hand back over my mouth. Hugo Bertram was one of nature's true gentlemen, a landowner of repute and the kindest and most amiable of men imaginable, yet he was still far above me in any social scale. Having Mr Bertram's permission to use his first name was something I had never expected. 'Sarah would be acceptable,' I managed to say.

'In that case, Sarah,' Hugo took my hand, 'you deserve a kiss.'

I proffered my lips but instead Hugo kissed the back of my hand, *a la France*, taking the time to comment on my most splendid ring.

The meal was excellent although I must say the meat was a trifle underdone. My Mother did not approve, as one glance at her face told me. I gave her a smile, to which she responded without in the least being able to hide the glisten of tears in her eyes.

'Time to cut the cake,' Mother announced with false gaiety.

There was a round of polite applause as William lifted the cake from the top table and had two servants carry it to the longer table further down the room. Naturally everybody gathered around to watch. I flinched as William suddenly drew his sword, and wondered if he had suddenly gone crazy or was he merely going to slice up a few of our guests to clear a space around the cake. However, it was neither as he soon explained.

'There is a tradition in the Regiment,' William said, 'that when the commander of the company gets married, he must cut the cake with the sword.'

'When did that tradition start?' A spotty young ensign asked.

'Right this minute,' William flourished his sword, with the long silver blade glittering in the light of a hundred candles. 'Stand back, ladies and gentlemen!'

The ladies and gentlemen all stood back, as did the people of lesser status. At that time I was not sure in which group I belonged; I did know that I was as happy as I ever had been with William; I did not know that the feeling was only temporary and would never come again.

'William,' the voice was low and deep, 'did you get another stone for my ring?' I did not know the tall woman who walked through the guests straight toward my husband.

Chapter Twenty-One

'Amelia?' I had never seen William look so startled; or so guilty. 'What are you doing here?' He glanced around him, 'you should not be here.'

'William,' I said, 'who is this woman?' She was about thirty, with an angular, arrogant face and clothes that might suit a governess or a duchess who cared little for the opinion of anybody else.

'This woman,' Amelia spoke in a voice that could crack glass, 'is Mrs William Chadwick. And who pray, are you?'

I felt as if the bottom had fallen out of my life for a second time. In that instant I knew that my marriage was doomed yet I straightened up and faced Amelia eye-to-eye. 'I am also Mrs Chadwick,' I said, 'I am Mrs William Chadwick.'

Her slap took me by surprise. My return slap astonished her. To judge by her reaction she had not expected me to retaliate; perhaps nobody had ever hit her before in her life. I did not mind being the first. She squealed and recoiled, holding her face with both hands.

'William!' I faced my husband, 'what is the meaning of this? Who is this woman?'

As William stared at me with his mouth open and his cake-smeared sword looking so silly in his hand, Mr Howard's voice broke what was a very awkward silence. 'This woman, the woman that you just slapped, is Captain William Chadwick's wife, Mrs Amelia Chadwick.'

'Oh,' I said. I would have apologised for slapping her if she had not hit me first. As the full realisation of Mr Howard's words hit me, I said: 'If that is William's wife then what about me?'

Mr Howard shook his head. 'I am very sorry, Miss Bembridge, or rather Mrs Baldivere, you are not married to William Chadwick. This lady is the Captain's first, real and only wife. Bigamy is not legal in Great Britain.'

I stared at him in incomprehension. I was aware of all the people around me, of the white faces staring at me and the mixture of malice and sympathy from officer's wives and true friends, yet I felt entirely alone in that crowded room. Truth to tell I felt as if the Mrs Bertram of the portrait was watching me, her eyes seeming to grow in size the longer I stood there in my misery. At last I spoke:

'Bigamy?' I said in a very small voice that nevertheless sounded like the blare of a trumpet within a locked closet.

'I am afraid so,' Mr Howard said. At that moment I could not have hated that man more if he had been Boney himself. I already guessed that he had searched for, located and brought the first Mrs Chadwick to my wedding, although I thought then it was out of pure wickedness.

'So I am not Mrs Chadwick?' I said as my dreams of the future crumpled into dust. I was not to be a captain's wife; I was not to hold court at regimental balls and functions; I was not to have dominion over these sharp-nosed, critical women with their expensive gowns; I was not to travel to places as exotic as Dublin, Edinburgh and London. I was to remain an inn-keepers daughter in the Back of Wight, skivvying for fishermen and drunken smugglers.

'Nor ever will be,' Amelia Chadwick said with utter malignance. Stepping closer, she wrestled the ring from my finger. 'I will have my ring back, if you please, madam.'

I did not resist. How could I? I stood there with the hot tears running down my face and my life in tatters as the officers' wives made their exit, sweeping their gowns aside as if touching me would soil them.

'I am sorry,' Mr Howard said. I saw him lift a hand as if to comfort me, but I was not to be comforted. How can one be comforted when one's whole future has collapsed and one's dreams and aspirations have been proven a sham?

I saw Amelia Chadwick hustle her husband outside and knew she was railing at him, yet I cared not a damn. I knew he may be prosecuted for bigamy and his career would be ruined; the name and reputation of his regiment would suffer and his life would never be the same again yet that did not matter. I saw my mother step toward me and I ran. I did not want sympathy; I did not wish for help; I had no care for soft words and soothing arms. I wanted only what I could never have. Instead I ran outside Knighton Hazard, past the chapel of so much heart-break, past the folly to woman's folly in choosing a poor husband and up to the Downs. There was only one place where I could find peace.

I sat in the shelter of the Long Stone with my wedding dress clinging to me in the soft rain and the Downs stretching around me, mute and quiet save for the sounds of nature. Twice now I had viewed the future with hope and twice fate had played a cruel trick that robbed me of happiness.

At that moment I was as close to despair as I ever had been in my life. Despite the beauty of the day, despite the host of butterflies that played around me, despite the liquid calling of the birds and the soft hushing of the wind, I could see nothing but bleakness. I do not know how long I was there. I only know that sometime later, maybe hours, maybe days, Molly found me and led me to her cottage.

'Bad times,' Molly said as she helped me out of my wedding dress and into more sensible clothing.

'Bad times,' I agreed. I noticed Charles standing in the background. He stepped toward me with his hand outstretched. His smile looked vaguely familiar although I did not have the inclination to pursue that thought. 'You're up, I see,' I said.

'You are down, I see,' Charles replied.

I tried to smile, failed dismally and felt my head spinning.

'I've got you, Sarah,' Charles said, as I fell into his arms.

It was two days before I returned to the Horse Head and the customers could not have been kinder. It is in times of duress that one really learns what people are like, and in my darkest times the people of the Back of Wight were there to support me. Mother, of course, was unchanging, working me like a dog and always there when I voiced about my troubles, while Mrs Captain Nash came in to offer silent sympathy and support.

When I think of that period of my life, there are no specific incidents that stand out. I remember talking to Mother about Mr Howard, and her listening to me while I called him every name I could think of in language that would have disgraced the most disreputable of marines. Mother listened without interruption and without mentioning my choice of words.

Eventually, when I had cursed myself dry, she put one finger under my chin. 'Now think, Sarah,' she said gently, 'how much worse it would have been if Mr Howard had not been suspicious of Captain Chadwick, and what might have happened if he had not prevented the wedding being consummated. You could have been the mother of an illegitimate child, born out of wedlock. That would have been a burden that followed you all of your life, a woman with no reputation except bad. You would never have found a respectable man then, or found a decent life.'

I stared at her, unwilling to accept that the man I had learned to hate with such ferocity may have in fact been helping me, in his own way. I humphed at that and stormed away with my head held high and my boots stomping on the floor. It was only after much reflection that I knew Mother was correct, and although I never admitted my mistake, I knew that she knew I had recognised the fact. After that I was able to be nearly civil to Mr Howard again. There was no need to be civil to Captain Chadwick and the Volunteers as they did not return to the Horse Head. Their custom was missed but not their company and I hoped that the people in Dublin treated them as they deserved. I did not know that my path, and that of Captain Chadwick, was to cross again in the near future.

'Did you love him?' Molly asked me as she and I sat with Charles outside her cottage. It was midsummer now, with butterflies colouring the air and one of her goats nuzzling Charles for food.

'Did I love him?' I pondered that question, aware that Charles was paying more attention to me than to his four-legged companion. 'No, I can't say that I did. I liked him and admired him, but I don't think I loved him.'

'Well then,' Molly said. 'Best rid of him now than live in a loveless marriage.'

'Don't wives and husbands grow to love each other?' I asked.

'So they say,' Molly snorted, 'although in my experience they are more likely to grow apart when the reality of life bites. Either you love your man or you don't.'

I looked up at the swelling downs where fields of wheat swayed in unison to the swish of the breeze. 'Maybe you are right,' I said.

Charles looked at me and smiled.

'The sea is busy today,' Molly nodded to the Channel, where a battered looking brig ushered a small convoy past the Needles, those fascinating but wickedly dangerous rock stacks that act as a sea-mark on the south west coast of Wight. 'That's the second London-bound convoy today and I am sure I saw a flotilla thrust its topsails over the horizon an hour past.'

'Maybe they expect Boney to come tonight.' I looked at Charles. 'Do you know anything about that?'

Charles shook his head. 'I am not even sure that I am French,' he said in his so-attractive French accent. 'If they come, then the Navy will be ready for them.'

'I hope so,' I said, honestly.

Charles did not smile. 'It was a dirty trick Captain Chadwick played on you,' he said, 'giving you his wife's ring as a present and pretending to marry you.' He pushed the goat gently away. 'You are too good for him, Sarah.'

It was so unusual for Charles to give his opinion on anything that I could not help but stare at him. 'Well Charles, thank you. He is a gentleman though, and I am only an inn-keeper's daughter.'

Charles shook his head. 'No gentleman would act so,' he said, 'while you have always acted like a lady with me, and I have heard nobody say a bad word against you.'

'Not even Kitty?' I asked after a pause. One must always keep an eye on one's best friend after all, especially is she is named Kitty Chillerton.

'She has always praised you,' Charles said, 'when you were not here to hear her.'

That shut me up, I can tell you. I had always viewed Kitty as the best of rivals and the most double-faced of friends, and here she was being nice about me behind my back. 'Wonders will never cease,' I said, making light of things even while I wondered about this new revelation. First I was told that Mr Howard had acted out of kindness and not malice and now I learned that Kitty maybe even liked me after all.

'She was quite right in what she said,' Charles continued.

I could hear no more of this. I was not used to praise of any sort and did not know how to react. 'I don't wish to know.' I said.

Molly smiled. 'It might do you good to hear what others think of you,' she said.

I was already walking away. I had my own opinion of me and I would not have it altered by that of others, particularly that hussy Kitty.

Mr Howard was in the Horse Head when I arrived, sitting in his usual seat and having his usual fresh fish followed by his usual Vectis pudding. 'Good evening Sarah.' He looked at me oddly, 'how are you today?'

I told him I was well, and apologised for not being there to look after Chocolate.

'He does prefer your touch,' Mr Howard said, 'you have a way with animals.'

'Thank you,' I said, wondering why everybody was being so nice to me that day. 'You are looking more cheerful.'

Mr Howard smiled. 'I may have located that elusive smuggler,' he said, 'and tomorrow I have some friends arriving who are very good at finding people.'

I felt my heart give a great lurch at that. I had no desire to see Charles dragged away and hanged or whatever it was Mr Howard had in mind for him. 'Oh,' I said, foolishly before my wits collected themselves. 'Where do you think he may be?'

'After scouring the island from end to end,' Mr Howard said, 'I think I have located him in a cottage not far from here.'

'That is good,' I sat down at Mr Howard's side. 'Could you tell me where?'

'Not exactly,' Mr Howard said, 'but a patrol of Yeomanry was marching past Berry Hill when they saw a young man on his own, a stranger they said, or an Overner, as the locals called him.'

'I see,' I said, feeling sick. Molly's cottage was tucked into the side of Berry Hill; trust the Yeomanry to be passing just when Charles happened to be outside. 'I wish you joy of your search, Mr Howard.'

'Thank you.' I started when he put a hand on my wrist. 'How are you, Sarah, after your upset?'

I was not sure how to answer. 'I am better now, thank you.' I still found it hard to meet his gaze.

'I did not like to disrupt your wedding.' Mr Howard spoke urgently, as if my opinion of him mattered. 'I tried to locate Captain Chadwick's wife before things were out of hand. I did not wish to tell you before in case I was wrong.'

I nodded. 'It was not nice when it happened.' That hand was patting my sleeve.

'It could not have been at a worse time,' Mr Howard said.

'It could have been after I was with child,' I repeated what Mother had said to me and watched the slight surprise on Mr Howard's face.

He nodded slowly. 'That is something I had not considered. Well said, Sarah, and bravely said as well.'

'You did me a great kindness, Mr Howard,' I said, although the words nearly stuck in my throat. 'I have a great deal to thank you for.'

Mr Howard's hand was busily patting my sleeve. 'You have nothing to thank me for, my dear, nothing at all.'

Now, you may be wondering how I was feeling when Mr Howard, a man old enough to be my father, was treating me in such a manner. Well, I was not enjoying it very much, let me assure you. After David who was about six years older than me, then William who was twelve years older, having Mr Howard, at least twenty years older than me being a little too friendly did not please me greatly.

'That is twice you have had an unfortunate experience at a wedding,' Mr Howard reminded me. 'You will be wondering if fate is against you.'

'I have thought that,' I admitted, pulling my arm clear.

'There will be another man,' Mr Howard said, 'and a better one.'

I shook my head. 'I am not looking for another husband. Two in the one summer is enough for now, thank you.'

Mr Howard lifted his pot of ale. 'Perhaps there is a husband looking for you.'

For some reason I felt a shiver run down my spine. 'I doubt that, and I hope not, Mr Howard.' I tried to make it obvious that I was not interested in a man of his age as I stood up and answered the call of another customer. All the same I could feel him watching me as I bustled around the tap-room. I tried to ignore him yet at the same time there was something reassuring about his presence.

No, I told myself. He is far too old for me. And I was right to think that.

Chapter Twenty-Two

As I left the Horse Head that night, there was another of these Channel fogs blanketing sound and reducing visibility so an Overner would not know a tree from a chime and would probably fall over the edge of a cliff and break his neck were he fool enough to attempt to walk abroad. However I was a Caulkhead born of generations of Caulkheads so my blood and bone belonged to Wight as much as the island belonged to me. I moved quickly through the dark, hearing the rustle of my skirt and the hollow thump of my feet on the damp ground above the muted hush of the surf and the distant clamour of a bell as some ship signalled the change of watch.

Molly was waiting for me, with an anxious looking Charles standing behind her.

'Are you ready?' I hissed.

'We are,' Molly said. I could hear unfamiliar tension in her voice. 'I am sure there is somebody moving out there.'

I stopped to listen. There was silence except for a distant owl and the constant hush of the sea. 'I can't hear anything,' I said. 'It was probably a poacher.'

'I know all the poachers and how they move,' Molly said.

'Do you want to stay here?' I looked back the way I had come. I knew that mist distorted sound so that distant noises appear close. 'Remember that Mr Howard will be knocking on your door tomorrow.'

'No, he cannot stay here; it's not safe for Charles,' Molly said.

We had readied bundles of necessities to keep Charles comfortable in Limestone Manor and we hefted them onto our backs as we left Molly's cottage. Molly and I knew the way and kept Charles in between us to guide him over the rough farm tracks and smooth grassland of the Downs.

'Don't stray,' I warned him, putting a hand on his arm as we came to a stile.

'What's that?' Charles stopped as there was the sound of feet ahead and something loomed out of the mist. For a moment we stared into two sets of green eyes and then the creature lumbered noisily away, joined by others of its type.

'Only sheep,' Molly said. She sniffed the air. 'There is something abroad tonight; there is something not right in Wight.'

Now I am not normally a superstitious woman but when a born and bred Caulkhead, particularly one with a penchant for the spiritual like Molly, thinks that something is not right; then there is reason to worry. 'Let's get Charles safe to Limestone Manor.'

It was not a long journey; perhaps three miles across the Downs yet that night it seemed to last forever as we started and stopped at every sound. Molly's warnings had unsettled me so I walked with fear in my heart. I had expected to be reassuring Charles but instead it was Charles who acted as my support whenever I jumped at the sound of a sheep bleating or the creak and rustle of a nearby tree.

'It's all right, Sarah,' he said in his rich and so-exotic French accented voice. 'You are doing very well.'

It was a bit embarrassing to find a foreigner giving me encouragement as I walked across my own island, yet in a strange way I quite enjoyed it. I did wonder at his wide command of the English language while I knew nobody who spoke French at all. Except Mr Howard of course, and that thought sliced off at a tangent. Charles had a strong accent while Mr Howard's English was flawless. If anything Mr Howard even had an English accent, not quite Wight- it might be Hampshire perhaps, which is the nearest mainland county to the island.

The voices sounded, faint but distinct through the mist. 'Sshh!' Molly touched my arm and we stopped. As luck would have it we were on a bare slope of the downs with nary a tree or wall to shelter behind. A treacherous gust of wind thinned the mist so we were alone and exposed with only the dark of a summer night to conceal us.

The voices sounded again.

'They're speaking French!' Molly glanced at Charles. 'It could be your friends looking for you.'

Charles frowned. 'I wish I knew who I was and where I was from,' he said. 'It is terrible not knowing anything about myself.' He lifted his head slightly to try and hear what was being said. 'I cannot make sense of the words. Something about a rendezvous, I think.'

I glanced at Molly. 'We'll get Charles safely in the Manor and then run and tell everybody that the French have landed. They must have slipped past the Navy in the mist.'

'That would be the squadron I saw hovering on the horizon,' Molly said. We waited for a few moments while my heart hammered fit to burst and Charles held my hand. 'The French seem to have gone now, let's get Charles safe.'

If anything the mist thickened as we approached Limestone Manor, so that it took all our local knowledge to recognise even the most obvious of landmarks as Molly brought us to a section of the boundary wall that sheep had tumbled down. Lifting her skirt nearly knee-high, she was first over, with me next and Charles last. He was still unsteady on his legs, stumbling a little on his damaged ankle as he negotiated the moss-slippery stones. I gave him my arm, which he took in a firm hand and together we walked cautiously toward the great manor house itself.

'We found you the most comfortable room that we could,' I spoke softly lest my voice carry in the mist. 'It is not as nice as Molly's cottage, but a lot safer if Mr Howard is looking for you.'

Charles reached for my hand and squeezed it. 'I cannot say how grateful I am for your help,' he said. 'You have been magnificent.'

'Oh, nonsense,' I said, looking away and withdrawing my hand lest he decided to keep it as a token of my help. I stopped in sudden fear. 'Oh my Lord!'

They loomed ahead, huge figures that seemed to rise from the ground. I tried to control my fear. If these were Frenchmen then they made even the tallest of our Guards seem like dwarves as they stood in front of us, silent and immobile.

'It's all right,' Charles took hold of my hand again. 'They're not real.'

'What?'

I had never been to this part of Limestone Manor's grounds as I normally entered from the main gate, so did not know what to expect. Now I saw that what I had thought were giant French soldiers were actually huge statues. I had to stifle a nervous giggle as I looked closer: they were statues of naked men and women in all manner of interesting poses.

'My word,' Molly pointed out a particularly well-endowed example of male humanity. 'I doubt they could find a fig-leaf large enough for that one.'

I giggled like a little school-girl. 'Maybe they are all that size in France,' I said and, despite myself, I looked toward Charles.

'Oh no,' he said at once. 'We don't show off the small specimens like that.' He glanced down at himself, then at me, and smiled.

'Oh!' I felt my mouth open in scandalised delight. Then I remembered that I had seen him in all his glory that night he had been cast ashore on our beach. 'Oh you are nothing like that,' I said, seeking to prick his male vanity.

Charles' smile did not falter. 'You only saw me after I had been immersed in cold water,' he reminded. 'I was not at my best.'

I nearly burst out laughing at that sally and only controlled myself with an effort. Luckily I recognised my reaction as the beginnings of nervous hysteria. 'We have to get into the manor,' I said, as inwardly I resolved to bring Kitty here so I could amaze her with what men could look like.

The side door was ajar and hung on a single hinge. Molly pushed it open and we filed out of the misty dim and into the musty dark. I had not thought to bring a lantern, but Molly was better prepared with three candles and a tinder box. We stood within the door for a nervous few moments as Molly scratched out a spark, and soon the flickering yellow glow of the candles pooled around us.

'This has been a grand place at one time,' Charles said.

'It's been crumbling for years,' I told him. 'More important is to get you to safety and then warn somebody that the French are about.' I paused as a new, unwelcome idea hit me. 'Unless you want to go and find the French? They would certainly take care of you.' I suddenly knew that I did not want him to go home. Looking at him through the flickering candle-flames, I felt a surge of affection for this Frenchman that we had rescued from the sea and cared for these past months.

'No,' Charles said. 'No: I don't want that.' I saw his monkey-face twist into something that was not quite a smile. 'I don't know what I want.' His eyes narrowed, possibly because I held my candle too close and the smoke nearly blinded him. 'Come on you two,' Molly said. 'Let's get Charles somewhere safe.'

We moved deeper into the house and up a flight of marble steps, with a marble balustrade well decorated with cobwebs from which palm-sized spiders scuttled away from the light of our candles. This wing of the house was two storeys high and when we reached the upper floor a panelled corridor ran the full length of the house and off which eight doors opened. I had selected the end room, partly because it was in the best condition, partly because it had a view along the bay toward the Horse Head Inn but mainly, I think, because there was a servant's entrance right next door with a flight of stairs leading all the way down to the servants' quarters in the basement.

'We cleaned it up for you,' I said as I pushed the door open. 'It's not as good as I would like.'

'Sarah means that *she* cleaned it up for you,' Molly said. 'I had nothing to do with it.'

'Sarah is very kind,' Charles said. I ignored his words.

The room was small and square with a single window, one of the few in the house that still retained every pane of glass. There was a large brass bed in one corner and a heavy carved chair in the other. Apart from that the room was empty.

We put down our bundles. 'There are no amenities,' I said as delicately as I could. 'So I found a chamber pot down stairs and slid it under the bed. You will have to do the emptying and cleaning yourself.'

'I am sure I can manage,' Charles said solemnly although I am certain I saw a twinkle of humour in his eyes. The best of men can be a little reticent when talking of such natural functions in the presence of ladies. Others are merely crude and offensive.

'We have brought bed covers, food and water,' Molly said. 'Either Sarah or I will call round every day to make sure you are all right, and to see if you have remembered who you are, Charles Louis Durand.' She glanced at me with a most curious expression on her face. 'I'm afraid I must hurry away now. I'll leave Sarah to make sure you are comfortable.' Touching Charles on the shoulder, she slipped out of the room and without another word she left by the servant's stairs.

Surprised by Molly's sudden departure, I was temporarily bereft of conversation, which is most unlike me. I do so like to talk you know. Left alone with Charles in Limestone Manor, I could only smile to him.

'You have chosen a fine room for me,' he said eventually. 'It is certainly most comfortable.

I looked around the room with its fancy plastered ceiling, empty fireplace and sparse furnishings. 'It is a shell of a place,' I said, as blunt as my mother.

'Thank you for your help.' He touched my arm, lightly before pulling away as if I was red hot.

I smiled. 'It is nothing.'

'You saved my life and cared for me, an enemy, for weeks,' Charles said. 'It is hardly nothing.'

For some reason I felt very embarrassed at this attention. 'Oh don't be silly,' I said, somewhat testily and turned away. 'Now; we've brought you food and water to keep you alive for a few days. There is a complete cooked chicken and sufficient apples and vegetables to feed an army.' Trust Mother to supply the food, despite her moans about the cost and losing money. Her complaints were meaningless; she could not help herself.

At a loss what to say, I stepped across the room. 'It is a fine bed,' I said, 'solid as the Rock of Gibraltar. We could not find a new mattress so filled bags with straw... 'I was talking nonsense now as I delayed leaving Charles alone. Why? He was only a shipwreck survivor, some stray seaman who would soon be returning to France. Yet he would leave quite a large hole in my life.

'Keep yourself hidden,' I said abruptly. 'And watch out for the French.'

'I don't have to,' Charles said. 'I think they are already here. Listen.'

Chapter Twenty-Three

The voices came to me from below, French and very nasal, frighteningly foreign as we stood in that small room.

'They are in this house,' I said as my heart began to pound most unpleasantly. 'I've brought you from the British frying pan into the French fire.'

'Sshh,' Charles blew out the candles. 'Keep quiet and keep still. Sound travels upward easier than downward so it is possible that they have not heard us yet.'

I was not happy in the sudden dark with the knowledge that there were French soldiers beneath us.

The sound of French voices increased as somebody barked a succession of what could only be orders. There was a whiff of tobacco and something else.

'Garlic,' Charles whispered. 'Most definitely French: keep still and keep silent.'

'What do we do now?' I wondered.

'We sit tight and hope they go away,' Charles' hand sought mine and squeezed reassuringly. 'It will be all right,' he said and added, 'it's not your fault.'

His words did not help. I had chosen Limestone Manor as a place to hide so it was my fault he had walked right into the arms of the French. I looked out the window, seeing only the Channel mist. There were no friendly lights from Brighstone, Chale or Blackgang; nothing but that clinging grey mist that, added to the dark, obscured everything. We had lived with the threat of French invasion for so long that it had become just part of life, yet secretly I had thought that the Royal Navy would be able to deal with any incursion before it happened, as Admiral Duncan had done in 1797. Now the unthinkable had happened and I felt nothing but fear.

His hand tightened around mine. 'It will be all right,' Charles said.

I nodded, fully aware that he could not see me in the dark. I wanted... I did not know what I wanted. I only knew that this situation was bad and may soon get worse. There were heavy footsteps on the stairs, the sound of somebody stumbling and what sounded like a curse.

'*Merde!*'

'Time to leave,' Charles made the decision for us both. Without another word he opened the room door and checked the corridor outside. 'Nobody there: come on!' Ushering me out, he pushed open the door of the servant's stairs and glanced down.

All I could see was darkness, yet that was far more inviting than the prospect of being discovered by the French. All the stories of rape and slaughter returned to me as I became once more the young Caulkhead and no longer the twice-married woman.

I was first through that door and waited for Charles. I heard a rough male voice shouting something, quickly followed by the sound of a blow.

'Charles,' I hissed, 'hurry! The French are coming.'

'It's all right, Sarah,' he said, 'I'm here.'

He sounded so different from the diffident young man who had occupied the bed in Molly's house that I scarcely recognised him.

'What happened?' I asked.

'There was a Frenchman.' Charles said. He showed me a pistol, dimly seen in the dark.

'What happened?' I repeated, grabbing his arm. 'Are you all right?'

'I seem to be,' Charles said. 'It was just instinct. I hit him: I seemed to know exactly what to do.' He pushed the door shut behind us. 'Now let's get away from here; there are more of these damned French about.'

That was the first time I had ever heard Charles swear. I also thought it was not the best time to remind him that he was also French.

'I'll lead,' Charles took command as if he had been born to it, holding his pistol muzzle-up as he negotiated the dark stairs one step at a time. Even as I descended I compared the cold stone steps and bare stone walls of these servants' stairs with the marble masterpiece we had ascended only a few short moments ago. The contrast was indicative of the alteration our lives had undergone: then I had viewed our situation as something of a game, an adventure, now I was in fear of my life, or worse, and rather than helping Charles, he was leading me.

'Here we are.' Charles said.

We had reached the foot of the steps and entered the servant's quarters. They were stifling dark and smelled of must and damp.

'We can either hide down here or get out of the house and as far away from the French as possible,' Charles looked at me, his face only a faint blur in the dark. 'I suggest we get away.'

'You might be discovered,' I said.

'I'll take my chance on that,' he replied without hesitation. 'It is more important to get you to safety.'

About to speak, I closed my mouth and said nothing. Our situations seemed to have been reversed. Charles had taken charge, and was doing it rather well, I thought.

We left that wing of the house far faster than we had arrived, passing the naked statues without a glance or a word as Charles led us back out of the policies of Limestone Manor.

I started as somebody shouted after us, the words unknown to me, distorted by the mist.

'They're chasing us,' I heard the fear in my own voice as I looked over my shoulder. 'I can see them!' They were shadowy figures with their shapes and sizes distorted so they could have been giants or dwarves, fat or thin, man or woman even, as if any army would ever recruit women into their ranks. Imagine men and women in the same regiment. What fun and what trouble that would cause. But I digress.

'They might shoot at us,' I sounded as scared as I was for, in truth, this was a brand new experience, being chased by Frenchmen on my own island.

'They won't,' Charles said. 'Even in this mist the sound of a musket will travel far and attract attention.'

'People will imagine that it's only a poacher,' I said.

'A musket sounds different from a fowling piece,' Charles was quite definite as we hurried away over the downs, careless of any sheep we disturbed.

Suddenly my fear vanished, to be replaced by a terrible all-consuming anger at these invaders. 'How about a pistol?' I said. I could hear the French pounding after us, their boots heavy on the ground. 'Would people recognise a pistol shot?'

'That's different again,' Charles said.

Although part of me wondered how he knew these things, most of me was so filled with anger that I pushed the thought from my mind. 'Will it bring the army here?'

The French were closing. I could hear their footsteps clearly now and even the harsh sound of a man's breathing, terrifyingly close through the mist. At that moment of my life I hated the French with more force than I have ever hated anybody or anything in my life; even more than I had hated Mr Howard at my last wedding, or Kitty when she stole young Thomas Smith from me and kissed him right before my eyes. I had been ten years old then ... but you do not wish to hear that just now.

'A pistol shot might well attract somebody's attention,' Charles said.

'Then give me that!' I snatched the pistol from Charles' grip and pointed it toward the patch of mist and darkness from where the nearest footfall came. As an inn-keeper's daughter I had often had occasion to take pistols from the belts of unconscious or just drunken patrons, but I had never fired one before. Without a qualm, I pressed the trigger and there came a tremendous roar and a kick that knocked me backwards. I felt as if my wrist was broken as Charles jumped to catch me as I fell. Charles won by a short head and grabbed me before I hit the ground. I have no idea where the pistol went for I certainly never saw it again.

Temporarily blinded by the muzzle flare and deafened by the noise, I coughed in the reek of powder smoke. 'That should bring the troops.'

'Up you get,' Charles helped me regain my balance.

'Did I kill anyone?' Strangely, that possibility only occurred to me now.

'Not unless they were flying in the air,' Charles pulled me on.

To judge by the sudden outbreak of barking, the sound of the gun had woken half the dogs in the area. Dim through the mist, I saw the glimmer of lights appear that must have been candles or lanterns as households awoke.

'Now stop,' Charles took hold of my shoulder. 'Right here.'

I did as he ordered. 'Why?' I hissed, inquisitive as always.

'Lie down,' He said urgently, 'and keep still.'

Once again I obeyed. It felt as if Charles had spent his life giving orders; he seemed a natural leader. 'Why? What's happening?'

He shushed me to silence and placed a hand across my mouth to ensure I stayed that way. We were in a shallow dip in the ground with the mist lying thick and clammy around us. I wanted to fidget, to rise and run as fast as I could as I heard men moving all around.

Unspeaking, they drifted past; I did not know how many there were, maybe half a dozen, maybe more. I only saw vague shapes in the mist, heard furtive movement and smelled them as they passed. I had never realised until that moment that Frenchmen have their own distinctive smell, like animals do. It was a combination of tobacco and garlic, with a whiff of something else. Foreign, I called it.

Charles had never smelled like that, I thought. Perhaps that was because he had been naked when first we found him. It is strange how these irrational thoughts race through one's mind at times of danger.

There was a sudden rift in the mist and in a gleam of moonlight I distinctly saw one of the Frenchmen. He was wearing the dreaded blue uniform of Bonaparte's soldiers, with white breeches and a tall shako-type hat. It was an image that I hoped never to see in my island, made all the worse by the long musket he carried and the fact that I lay prone on the ground beside a man I had cared for some long weeks but barely knew. How could I know him when he did not know himself?

I shivered, and Charles' arm eased around me. He said nothing yet I knew that he would look after me even against men of his own nation. That was another epiphany: nationality was of less importance than people. It was something I had never thought to learn.

The French slithered into the mist as the gap closed and the light eased away. We were alone on that bare hillside.

Charles shook me gently, put a hand to his lips and rose, very slowly, to his feet. I followed, shaking and weak yet determined not to allow any blasted Frenchmen scare me to death.

There were other voices now, honest Englishmen shouting to each other; the renewed barking of dogs and crisp orders through the dark. I distinctly heard a voice shout 'what the devil is happening,' recognised Captain Chadwick's tones and wondered if I cared to meet him any more than I wished to encounter Boney's infantry. In my eyes, both were equally obnoxious.

'We should go to them,' Charles said softly.

'And have you arrested or shot?' I said. 'Certainly not!' I could be quite sharp when needed, you see. 'I have not wasted so many weeks of my life keeping you safe to have you stuck in some filthy prison hulk now just because a few blasted Frenchmen are visiting!'

'They won't know I'm French.' For some reason, Charles was smiling.

'Of course they'll know,' I snapped. Really, that man was trying my patience; or perhaps my nerves were jangling after the events of the night. 'As soon as you open your mouth they will hear your accent.'

'I cannot remember being French,' Charles said, until I interrupted his nonsense with a deep sigh.

'Well you are,' I said. 'It seems as if we are stuck between the devil of Captain Chadwick and the deep blue sea of Boney's men.' I was thinking rapidly, trying to work out what was best to do. I had intended hiding Charles in Limestone Manor until the inquisitive Mr Howard gave up his search and left the island, but the French landing had altered all my plans.

Would Mr Howard still be searching for one lone man while the French invaded? Or would other matters occupy his attention. I had a sudden start. Perhaps the invasion was the reason that Mr Howard was here! Maybe he had been preparing the ground for the French, mapping all the villages and getting to know the defences and searching for Charles was only an excuse. That thought was so sobering that I gasped.

'Sarah? Are you all right?' Charles was instant attention.

'Yes,' I said. 'Yes thank you.' I was not sure if I was or not. There were so many thoughts racing through my head that I was confused: I hoped that Mother was all right, yet I knew that to bring Charles back to the inn would be foolish indeed. On every occasion that the Volunteers, Militia or even the regular army had their silly soldier games, they used the Horse Head as a temporary base. It would be no different during the invasion. My home would be full of officers with their arrogance and braying accents, while their men would infest the surroundings, drinking, spitting, smoking and doing worse things that I can hardly bear to think of let alone write about.

I hoped that Mother was safe, yet I knew that if the End of all Things were to happen tomorrow, then the very next day that indomitable woman would crawl out from under the wreckage, tidy it all up and organise those who survived the carnage to create a new and better world. Pity help the Frenchman who tried to damage her inn or her customers. Pushing that thought to the recesses of my mind, I wondered where else I could leave Charles while I found out what was happening in the island.

'Listen,' I said, 'can you hear anything?'

Charles shook his head. 'Not since that fellow Chadwick stopped shouting,' he said.

'Maybe we are safe to move,' I said.

'Where are we going? Back to Molly's cottage?' Charles looked around. The night was easing into dawn but the fog remained, hampering visibility so I could hardly make out the nearest tree yet alone see the progress of the invasion.

'Listen!' Charles put a hand on my sleeve. 'Musketry!'

It was distinct. I had heard the first report without registering it; now I heard others. Two muskets fired together; then a third, followed by an irregular volley and then another, solitary shot. A voice called through the mist, the words indistinct and the tone hoarse.

'Did you see the muzzle flashes?' Charles asked.

'I did not,' I admitted.

'Nor did I. They may be some distance off then, or merely hidden in a dip of the hills.' Charles sounded quite casual.

'Have you done this sort of thing before?' I asked, and added, greatly daring, 'are you another French spy, Charles, come to prepare the island for the invasion?'

'I wish I knew,' he said. 'What do you mean by another French spy? Do you have many French spies walking the Downs of Wight?'

'Mr Howard is the only one I know of,' I said.

'I see.' Despite our predicament, Charles managed to smile. 'Well, perhaps that is why he is searching for me, to ascertain what information I have found out.'

'And what information have you found out, Mr Durand? Or should that be Monsieur Durand?' I put some venom into my voice for if the truth be told I was finding it rather wearisome sitting on wet grass in the middle of a misty field with Frenchmen and Chadwicks and God-only-knew-what other men searching for me and firing their silly muskets all night long. I mean, a girl has other things to do except dodge strange men all her life.

'Plain old-fashioned mister will do me, I think,' Charles did not lose his smile. Honestly that man had the patience of a saint; or perhaps the patience of a French spy. 'I have found out that Wight women are amongst the most kind and amiable in the land,' he said, 'and one in particular has quite stolen my heart.'

'Molly has a way of doing that,' I said, suddenly tart. 'She knows how to mix herbs and potions to make people do as she desires. Her father was a vicar and I have heard that her mother was a witch. Aye, I quite believe it.'

'Kitty also has that skill of charming men,' Charles said.

Now, if he had said that only a few days previously I would have had such a twist of jealousy I swear that I might have reported him to Captain Chadwick or even the French, such was my spite. However, after hearing that Kitty had said nice things about me behind my back I was not prepared to react in such a dramatic way. Instead I merely smiled, hated Kitty a little and took a small step further away.

'Kitty is well favoured in many ways,' I said. 'She has a countenance that many men find pleasing, Mr Durand. You would not be the first, you do realise.'

'A girl with the looks and charm of Kitty Chillerton will never lack for suitors,' Charles said. 'It will be a lucky man who wins her heart and hand and keeps them both secure and chaste to himself.'

'That will be a lucky man indeed,' I murmured. The thought of Kitty being chaste made me smile.

As I spoke I felt an unusual hollow sensation within me, as if I had made a discovery and lost it all within the same instant, or I had found a penny and lost a sixpence. I did not understand this new feeling; I only knew that I had never felt anything quite like it before. One part of me wanted to examine and savour it, another part wished to push it as far away as possible, for I knew that if it remained, I would not be the same Sarah Bembridge again in my life. I needed time and space to think, yet here I was encumbered by this monkey-faced Frenchman while more French infested the island with their damned garlic and roamed around as if they owned the place.

'I need to go to the Long Stone,' I said.

'Where is that?' asked Charles. 'Who is there?'

'I am there.' I was not being intentionally cryptic; my mind and emotions were in such a whirl that I am not sure how I managed to sound even half coherent.

Charles gave me an odd sideways-on look, as if he was wondering who this mad woman was. I ignored that and rose quickly. I was very aware that there were hundreds of Frenchmen running loose on the island but I did not care. I knew, somehow, that I would reach the Long Stone safely despite Boney and all his minions, and Chadwick and all his too, come to think of it, so I marched confidently across the Downs with Charles a step or two behind me and the mist very gradually thinning out.

Once I reach the Long Stone, I told myself, all would be well. Things would work out, I would find the answers and the world would right itself. I had great faith, not in the power of that stone, for it is only a great chunk of rock set upon a hillside, but in the power of … of what I did not know. I only knew that once I reached my own favourite spot in all of Wight, something would happen.

It may have been fate, or luck, or just something that happened, but a gap had formed in the mist so the Long Stone stood erect in a clearing like a broad shouldered man, with the second, recumbent stone lying at his feet.

Charles looked around him as if expecting to see a house or an inn or some other sign of civilisation. 'What is this?'

'The Long Stone,' I told him quietly. 'It is my own special place.' I did not want to mention that I had brought David and William here within the last few months. Perhaps this stone was unlucky, rather than lucky.

'What is it?' Charles sounded puzzled. 'I have seen something similar before.' Reaching out, he touched the stone. '*La Longue Rocque*,' he said. 'It is like *La Longue Rocque*.'

I felt something sink within me. All this time I had thought of Charles as being French but I had hoped that somehow he would remember something that proved he was not. True, his first words had been French but he also spoke perfect English enhanced by that delightful accent, and now at last when he remembered something, it was French he spoke again.

'Can you remember where this La Long Rock place is?' I asked, knowing that I did not wish to hear the answer but equally desperate to know the truth.

As Charles looked at me I saw the confusion in his eyes. 'I don't know,' he said and I swear he was as close to tears as I ever saw him. 'I don't know.' He ran his hands over the surface of the Long Stone as if it was an old friend, or a horse perhaps.

'Was it in France?' I pressed, hating myself for hurting him. 'Was it in Brittany? Are you a Breton? Or maybe Normandy? Are you from Calais perhaps? Do any of these names mean anything to you?'

Charles shook his head helplessly. 'No,' he said, 'they are only names. I remember the *La Longue Rocque* though. It is a stone like this one, and there is another smaller stone nearby.'

'Where are these stones?' I took hold of his shoulders and shook him. In my fear and frustration I nearly slapped him and perhaps that may have helped. I know that is what my Mother would have done if I had exasperated her so, but she knew me well, you see, and I did not know Charles well at all. If I had I would have slapped him hard as I could to shock the truth out of him and I swear we would have both laughed at it afterward.

Instead we stared at each other for a long minute before I took his hand. 'Don't take it too hard,' I said, feeling sick. 'It will come. You had one returned memory today. There are bound to be more and then, eventually you will re-member everything once more.' I gave him my best impression of a confident smile. 'I wager you have a lovely French wife to go back home to.'

'Oh I am not married,' Charles said at once.

'You are sure of that?' I asked.

'Why yes,' he said. 'I have only ever had one sweetheart and she...' He shook his head. 'She went away with another man,' he said softly. 'There was a fight. Some sort of fight.' He shook his head again.

'Well then,' I could see he was upset and there is only one cure for an upset handsome young man. 'If you have no sweetheart, not even Kitty Chillerton, then there is nobody to complain if I do this.' And I kissed him.

To this day I do not know why I did that. There was nothing in his attitude to suggest any attraction to me, quite the reverse if his earlier statement about Kitty were to be believed, and I did not find him nearly as handsome as David or William. As far as future security was concerned my monkey-faced Frenchman had come into my life with only his naked skin and an addled head.

I stepped back, not sure if I had offended him, scared of my own actions and so embarrassed that I felt my face flushing as scarlet as the tunic of any Volunteer officer.

Charles put one hand to his lips. 'Sarah,' he said, so quietly that I had to strain to hear him. 'I have been hoping you would do that since I opened my first opened my eyes and thought you were an angel.'

'I am no angel,' I said, equally softly. 'Just a Caulkhead girl.' I tried to smile. 'I thought you would prefer a kiss from Kitty? A Kitty-kiss?'

'Not even a catty-kiss,' Charles said.

We were both speaking very quietly, uncaring of the mist that swirled around us, making the Long Stone the eye of a grey-white vortex that seemed to consume the entire island. At that moment were alone; the rest of the world did not matter. We lived in our own small, yet to us vitally important world.

We did not say much as our lives changed forever. Leaning forward, I kissed him again, this time without any doubt. I was not kissing him to reassure him, or to make him feel better; I was kissing him because I wanted to kiss him, and, to judge by his response, he had no objections to being kissed.

I pulled back again, with my heart hammering within me and my eyes wide open. I touched my lips with my fingers, and then touched his. 'Charles,' I said, and stopped. I did not know what I felt, yet alone what I should say.

He nodded. 'Yes,' he said.

'What is this?' I asked.

He shook his head and shrugged like a Frenchman. 'I don't know.'

I think we both knew. I also think we were reluctant to admit what we thought and how we felt. All around us the mist continued to swirl, blocking out the world. I had forgotten all about the French and the Volunteers and even Mr Howard as Charles held out his hand to me.

I took it, feeling the returning strength in his fingers, feeling the hardness of his muscles and the calluses at the base of each finger. 'Whoever you were,' I said, 'you were not a soft-living man. You have the hand of a seaman.'

The words were simple yet true. I had lived among men of the sea and men of the soil all my life. If I knew anything at all it was how to distinguish a man who worked with his hands from a man who did not. Charles had the hands of a seaman, hard and powerful from years of hauling ropes and wrestling canvas.

'*Les Hanois*,' Charles said at once. 'She is the finest vessel to sail the Channel.' He looked at me and repeated. '*Les Hanois*: that is the name of my ship.'

'That is a French name,' I said.

'I fear so,' Charles said sadly. 'Yet she was named after something else. I cannot think what.' He shook his head violently. 'Oh this is so maddening!'

'Never mind,' I said quickly, unwilling to break the mood, or the bond that I had felt was forming between us. 'You got another name and you remembered you were a seaman; that is good.'

'I want to know more,' Charles said, so I kissed him again.

At first he did not respond, so I slipped my hands around him, feeling the wiry strength of him and remembering how he had looked when first I saw him. Unable to help myself, I pulled him closer. He responded, with his arms closing around me in the most delightful way possible. Suddenly rather than me holding him, our positions were reversed and he was holding me, supporting all my weight and then he kissed me. His hands were busy on my back, insistent, caring, gentle as they caressed.

'Dear Lord,' I said as we slid to the ground beside the Long Stone. The grass was damp, the stone cool yet friendly as Charles' hands explored the outside of my legs and further up, smoothing over my hips and up my flanks to my breasts.

'Charles,' I said, softly, hopefully, pushing into him as he looked down on me. His eyes were soft with love as they met mine and I knew then that my two previous men had not been right for me. David had been a young man with an urge and William an adulterer looking for a younger woman. This man, this French seaman, this Charles Louis Durand, was my present and my future; this man was to be my husband and to the very devil with national boundaries, kings, queens, republics and anything else that acted as a barrier to what was undoubtedly, indisputably, unquestionably, right.

I had known that things would work out at the Long Stone and they had, even if not at all in the way that I had expected.

'Charles,' I said, and then I said nothing coherent for quite some time as we proved our love for each other at that ancient, beautiful place.

The mist was clearing as we lay together with his arms folded around me and my head pillowed on his chest. 'I wonder what this place was for,' Charles murmured. 'Maybe some religious site, a temple of the druids or a place to worship the sun or the moon.'

'That may be so,' I snuggled closer. Yes it was damp all around us but when one is in love the weather really does not matter, does it? You see that I used that word *love* again. By that time I knew that I was in love with Charles, in a way I had not been in love with either David or William. This was real; it was something that came from deep within me and with a certainty that precluded all others. I thought, briefly, of Mr Howard's clumsy attempts to woo me and was very glad that I had not entered the path he so artfully laid.

'I love you,' I made it official.

'I have loved you since the first minute I saw you,' Charles told me. 'I did not know how to say it.'

His arms tightened around me. It was secure within these arms. They were strong, muscular, protective; the arms of a man. I wanted to stay there and be nowhere else, ever.

'People will not like us being together,' I said.

'I don't care,' Charles said.

'They will make it difficult for us,' I said.

'That will only make our love stronger,' Charles grip was unflinching.

'Mr Howard wants me as his wife, I fear.'

'Than I will eat Mr Howard,' Charles was becoming a little outrageous in his statements. 'Or challenge him to a duel.'

'I would rather you did not do that,' I said. 'I quite like Mr Howard, despite the fact that he is a French spy and wants to throw me over his shoulder and carry me off to Paris with him.' I had a sudden vision of Mr Howard doing exactly that, with my legs kicking as I perched across his shoulder and all the people in the Back of Wight waving as I was carried out of the chapel. I could see these two portraits watching me, Mr and Mrs Bertram, both wearing completely opposed clothes and living utterly different lives.

'When they find out you are French they will come for you,' I said, more seriously.

'Then we will board my boat and sail away from Wight and England and France, we will escape from kings and queens and emperors and wars and governments.' These strong hands began moving on my person. I did not object to what they were doing.

'Would that be *Les Hanois*,' I asked.

''My beautiful *Les Hanois*,' Charles said, 'the fastest sloop between Brittany and the Scillies, able to ride the wind and smooth the storm gods with her figurehead.' He moved slightly beneath me. 'She has the most perfect figurehead,' he told me. 'Venus in all her glory with breasts that would grace a goddess...'

'I am not at all certain that I wish to hear this,' I said mildly. 'Is it a good idea to praise the breasts of another woman while fondling those that belong to me?'

Charles laughed. 'You would love her, Sarah.'

'And you remember her,' I said, gently.

'She is the love of my life,' Charles said, and quickly corrected himself. 'Or rather, she was the love of my life until I met you.'

'And one sight of me put her quite out of your head,' I allowed my left hand to do a little exploring of its own, tracing his muscular back and the deep ridge of his spine down, down, down with my finger stepping to more smoothly curving muscles, where they rested, kneaded and prepared for their next and even more daring adventure.

'If they catch you,' I said more seriously, 'they will put you in the hulks,' I said, testing him even as I hated the words I said.

'Then I will escape and swim to your island,' Charles told me. 'Or I will say I am a royalist and join you here.' He shrugged, 'for all I know that is true. I could well be a royalist, a rebel against Napoleon Bonaparte. *Vive le Roi.*'

He stopped suddenly. '*Les Hanois*,' he said. It is a reef; my vessel is named after a reef!' He grinned to me. 'I should say *Vive le Roi* more often.'

'*Vive le Roi*,' I repeated, softly. Even in such an insular country as England with our dislike of foreigners in general and Frenchmen in particular, we know that these three words meant. '*Vive le Roi*: Long Live the King!'

These words were the talisman that the royalist resistance against the Republican murderers had used since 1789. Now that Napoleon Bonaparte had usurped the Revolution for his own even more egoistical cause I could identify with the royalists with enthusiasm. In my sudden surge of royalism and maybe because of what had happened between me and Charles, I shouted the words with gusto and Charles, caught in the mood of the moment, joined in. Our combined voices yelled '*Vive le Roi!*' as we lay beside the Long Stone in the mist.

'*Vive le Roi!*' we roared, and then we realised that the mist no longer concealed us and we were not alone on Mottistone Down.

Chapter Twenty-Four

Before I continue I must explain that these ancient Stone raisers knew what they were about when they placed the Long Stone exactly where it is, for it commands one of the finest all-round panoramas in an island where extensive views are common. If we looked south and west we could see the headland of Hanover Point and the great sandy sweep of Compton Bay and Freshwater Bay all the way to Scratchell's Bay and the Needles. If we looked east we had the beautiful rolling downland, great hedged fields and patterned woods of the fertile interior of Wight. It is the finest spot in the island, and that means the finest spot in God's own garden, for Eden was surely planted here rather than in the heat and dust of somewhere East of Egypt.

Unfortunately, because it commands such spectacular views, the Long Stone is also highly visible. Charles and I had been so intent with each other that he had not noticed that the mist had drifted away so we were quite exposed beside the stone, while the noise that we were making had attracted some very unwelcome company.

'*Vive La Republique,*' one of the three French soldiers said quietly while his two companions merely stared at the spectacle of two near-naked people lying on damp grass beside a great hunk of stone. Naturally I scrambled up and hastened to cover myself, while Charles stepped forward manfully to protect me.

I am not sure what was said in the next few moments, except that it was in French, it was very loud and there were many hand gestures, both by the soldiers and by Charles, who gave every bit as good as he got, despite his handicap of having nothing covering his lower half and very little above that. However he did dress himself as he spoke and the soldiers were gentleman enough not to try and interfere as I did the same.

'They want us to go with them,' Charles said as he fastened his trousers.

'Where?' I looked around. There were more Frenchmen on the slopes of Mottistone Down, speckling the calm green with their invasive blue uniforms. 'I am not going!'

Unfortunately I had little choice in the matter. While two soldiers fixed wicked looking bayonets and prodded them at Charles, the third encouraged me to accompany him by the simple expedient of grabbing hold of my hair and dragging me behind him. My protests may have reached the mainland but they did not help my case in the slightest, and when Charles came to help one of the soldiers fetched him a blow with the butt of his musket that knocked him to the ground.

'Charles!' I reached for him, fruitlessly. 'All right,' I said. 'I'll come along.'

Holding his face where the musket butt had hit him, Charles said something and the soldier relaxed his hold on my hair. I scowled at him and moved closer to Charles. 'Are you all right?'

'Are you?' The musket had left a huge red mark that would undoubtedly turn into a bruise before long. If I had felt my first taste of real love with Charles only a couple of hours ago, now I felt absolute hatred for that Frenchman who had hurt my man. I did not know that I was capable of such deep loathing.

When I touched Charles' face he flinched. My anger boiled over. Unable to prevent myself, I landed a full force slap right across the face of the French soldier who had hit him. It was a beautiful slap, if I say so myself, and unbalanced the rogue. He staggered; Charles grabbed his musket, pushed me to one side and fired a single shot. The sound seemed to deafen me far more than the pistol had.

'Run!' Charles nearly screamed. 'Run Sarah, for your life!'

Glancing over my shoulder I saw him close with the remaining two Frenchmen.

'Run, Sarah!' Charles shouted.

I saw him duck under the bayonet thrust of the first Frenchman, saw him knock the man down with his own musket and stab him in the chest. Then I turned around to help him. I know that Charles had ordered me to run but I would not let him fight alone, even although I was scared near out of my wits.

I was not needed. Before I got close enough to help him, he had knocked the other Frenchmen down.

'I told you to run,' he grabbed me roughly and hustled me away from the scene. 'This is no place to linger.'

We ran, or rather Charles ran, dragging me behind him. I did not protest.

'That way,' I said, guiding him as best I could toward the Horse Head. 'The Army will be there.' I looked at him. 'You are no friend of the French now.'

He nodded. 'Come on then.'

I looked behind me. There were French swarming over my downs. They did not belong there. I hated seeing them there. 'Let's get to the Horse Head, Charles.'

There were small parties of Frenchmen scattered between us and the inn, but I knew the island better than they ever would. On our way we called at Molly's cottage, only to find her out, with the walls of her fields down and her goats scattered across the downs.

'I hope she is safe,' Charles said.

'I would not like to be the Frenchman who tried to hurt her,' I said, although I was not as certain as I tried to sound. I had been scared when the soldiers captured us; now I was sick at heart. Watching a hostile force take possession of all that is dear to you is worse than anything you can imagine. All I can say is: thank God for Mr Howard.

I told you at the beginning of this tale of mine that there was a fog the day he arrived, without telling you exactly who the 'he' was. Well, if you have read this far, then please finish the story and you will find out all.

I was flagging by this time. I tell you that men have it easy with their trousers and even breeches. Running with free legs such as that must be so much better than running in long clinging skirts. I had also been awake all night and moving most of it. Despite having spent weeks in bed, Charles seemed as fresh as if he had just woken up.

We reached the top of a knoll that gave us a most splendid view over the rolling hills and downs, with the small villages and hamlets, the isolated farms and cottages and the fields of wheat, sheep or cattle. I had been so intent on running that I had not noticed that the sun had quite burned away the mist and it was a really pleasant summer day. I also noticed that the French soldiers were beginning to form together; they were no longer scattered around the fields. There were men shouting at them, either officers or sergeants as they gathered in a single blue column.

'We don't need to go to the Horse Head to get the army, Sarah,' Charles said. 'The army is right over there. Unfortunately the French are between us.'

Chapter Twenty-Five

I am not sure what I expected. Probably I thought there would be two armies of brave men exchanging great volleys of musketry with heroic charges and deeds of derring-do by stalwart young heroes, or something of that nature. The reality was somewhat different.

The French had gathered all their men into a single column and marched across the fields with absolutely no regard for walls, hedges or the welfare of the livestock. As they marched a great double line of redcoats waited for them behind a screen of trees, with Captain Chadwick in the centre on his horse, sword in his hand and looking very martial and important. Despite myself I could not help smiling at the sight and wondering, just a little bit, what might have been. He looked … and I glanced toward Charles and pushed William Chadwick entirely from my mind.

'Stay with me,' Charles said. He nodded to our left. 'Look over there.'

Sheltering behind a straggling wood, there were more soldiers, standing silent in another line. Rank after rank of scarlet clad men. The two armies could not see each other because of the trees in between but from our elevated viewpoint we could see the whole panoply of battle, both British and French as the French moved forward at the slow pace of marching men. To my inexperienced eyes, it seemed as if the French were marching into a scarlet box with very thin sides.

'Who are they?' Charles pointed to a group of men who stood on tall horses at what would be the hinge of the British box. Two were obviously important military men in ornate scarlet uniforms much decorated with gold braid with a small number of more plainly uniformed horsemen who seemed to be waiting for orders. In the middle of the group was a tall civilian who I knew very well.

'That's Mr Howard,' I said. 'The French spy who is looking for you.'

'I know that man,' Charles face creased into a puzzled frown. 'I am sure that I should know that man.'

'He knows you as well,' I said.

'Whoever he is,' Charles said, 'he is not French. He seems to be helping to command the British forces. I don't believe that French spies do that.'

As the French column trod on, Mr Howard leaned toward the two senior officers and moments later two junior horsemen detached from the group and galloped away, one to either side of the British box. The redcoated soldiers advanced a few paces through a screen of trees and stopped on the other side, when they were fully visible to the French.

The French column came to a juddering halt as they realised they were all but surrounded by two British lines.

Charles took hold of my arm. 'If these fellows start to fight,' he said, 'we'll get to the other side of this hill and lie down flat.'

'I want to see,' I said.

'No doubt you do,' Charles said, 'but there will be an awful lot of musket balls flying around and I don't want you to get in the way of one of them.'

The two armies scanned each other in what was nearly perfect silence. Only the occasional cough from individual men and the neighing and whinnying of the horses disturbed the surreal hush.

'What is going to happen?' I whispered.

'I don't know,' Charles gripped my hand as if he was afraid it would fall off the end of my arm.

I saw Mr Howard speak to one of the senior officers, who sent more horsemen to both flanks of the British army. The scarlet lines moved forward slowly, keeping in that perfect silence save for the whisper of grass beneath their boots.

'Make ready!' The words were distinct, repeated from officer to officer. The British soldiers lifted their muskets so they were held at a 45 degree angle.

'Present!'

Both sides of the British box lifted their muskets to their shoulders, aiming at the French. There must have been around five hundred muskets aimed at the French column.

'Oh God,' I said, 'I don't want to see,' yet at the same time there was a fascination in watching this cruel game of war. 'What will happen next?'

The blue-clad column stood still as if unable to decide what to do. 'The French are in a bit of a quandary.' Although Charles spoke normally, his voice seemed to carry like a fog horn. 'If they remain as they are, the British lines will fire and there will be a massacre. If they advance, they will be closer to the British so the next volley will kill even more of them; if they retreat they will be caught in flank by that second British line.'

'Poor men,' I said. Suddenly the evil, tailed French ogres had become men no different to those that I knew, young men with mothers, married men with wives, family men with daughters and sons of their own.

'Wait...' Charles hand tightened even further around my own. 'Something's happening.'

Two horsemen trotted forward from the knot of British officers. One carried the white flag of parley, the other was Mr Howard.

'The French will slaughter them,' I said. Having been raised on tales of French perfidy I was prepared to believe anything of these evil foreigners from the other side of the Channel. Instead a mounted officer rode forward from the French ranks to meet Mr Howard.

'It's a trick,' I said. 'They'll kill him.'

'No they won't.' Charles soothed my fears. 'I think peace is about to break out.'

Charles was correct. As you will know from your history books, there never was a battle on the Isle of Wight. The French commander, presumably realising that to fight would only result in the needless slaughter of his men, shouted something out. There was a moment of silence and then we watched the French carefully pile their muskets in neat little pyramids as the British moved down to them. I had expected jeers and vituperation. Instead, while Chadwick's Volunteers watched from a short distance away with their muskets ready, the second British line, regular soldiers, moved among the French, shaking hands, exchanging tobacco and surreptitious sips from water bottles that certainly did not contain water and generally making friends.

'So what now?' I wondered. The battle and the French invasion of Wight had ended in an anti-climax, yet I was left with the same problem of what to do with Charles.

'I do know that man,' Charles said. 'Come on, Sarah. He might solve the mystery of who I am and what I am doing here.'

'Be careful, Charles,' I said.

'I have been careful long enough,' he told me, smiling. 'Somehow I think that this is the time to be bold. It seems more natural.'

Clutching his arm, I accompanied Charles down the slope and through what might have been a battlefield. Both British and French soldiers looked at us with surprise but nobody sought to block our path. One or two of the French made comments to me, although I do not know what they said. When Charles laughed, I suspected that the Frenchmen were being somewhat risqué but Charles refused to tell me and to this day I do not know.

Mr Howard was in the centre of a knot of officers, both British and French when we approached. Two stalwart soldiers moved toward us when we got close.

'Hey; where the devil do you two think you are going?' The first soldier had a face the colour of nutmeg and the three stripes of a sergeant.

'We are going to speak to Mr Howard,' I said as calmly as any woman could when she was surrounded by hundreds of men.

'Oh no you're not. 'The sergeant put a hand the size of a ham on Charles' chest. 'He's too important for the likes of you.'

'Do you know who we are?' Charles adopted a very lofty tone that I had never heard before.

'Some island peasant with big ideas,' the sergeant said. He nodded to his nearly-as-large companion who took hold of my arm, quite gently.

'Sorry miss; orders is orders,' the second soldier said.

'I am Charles Durand, just come from Limestone Manor,' Charles said truthfully in that impeccable accent. 'I am certain that Adam would wish to see me.'

'Adam?' The sergeant was slightly less sure of himself now.

'Adam Howard,' Charles said.

'Charles?' Mr Howard sounded incredulous. 'Charlie: is that you?' Ignoring the senior officers, both French and British that stood on either side of him, Mr Howard advanced on Charles with his arms outstretched. 'Charles; you're alive! Where have you been? I've been searching for weeks!'

As I watched, unable to restrain my smile, Mr Howard enfolded Charles in a tremendous hug that lasted at least two full minutes. 'Charles, my dear, dear boy.'

'I think they know each other,' the second soldier said to me, and repeated the words to the sun-tanned sergeant. 'They know each other.'

The other officers were equally pleased, nudging each other and exchanging murmured comments.

When at last Mr Howard released Charles he looked to me. 'Sarah my dear; you found him. I cannot thank you enough. What can I say? What can I do in return?'

My smile was probably a trifle uncertain. 'I think that Charles would like to know who he is,' I said. 'And what he is doing here. There are so many questions.'

Mr Howard started. 'He is Charles Durand, of course, Master of the sloop *Les Hanois* out of St Peter Port in Guernsey. He is my adopted son.'

Chapter Twenty-Six

We gathered in the tap-room of the Horse Head, me, Charles, Mr Howard, Molly, Hugo Bertram and Mother, all cosy beside the roaring fire and with brandy punch and rabbit stew in front of us as we mulled over the events of the past few weeks.

'So Charles is from Guernsey,' I said. 'That would explain why he speaks French so fluently.'

'He has grown up with both languages,' Mr Howard said, 'as have most of the population of that island.' His smile was more relaxed than I had ever seen.

I nudged Charles. 'If we had known that, we could have saved us all a great deal of trouble.'

'That is true,' Charles said, 'yet think of the stories we can relate.'

I coloured a little, 'yes, and the stories we will never repeat.' Realising that Mr Howard and my mother were both looking intrigued, I closed my mouth and said no more.

'So you really thought I was a French spy?' Mr Howard roared with laughter as I told him I had followed him to Limestone Manor that day so very long ago. 'Dear God in all his glory, I am the very opposite! I work for the British government.'

'I heard you speaking French to some people.' I had not forgotten that beautiful, elegant French woman or the other man who had been with Mr Howard that day.

Mr Howard supped at his punch. 'We were studying maps of tidal currents and places where this young man,' he patted Charles on the shoulder, 'could have come ashore. I never believed that he was drowned. He could always swim like a shark.'

Charles gave an uncertain smile. 'I am glad you found me, Father, yet I still do not remember. I have a name *La Longue Rocque*, in my mind, and the image of a very beautiful lady.'

'*La Longue Rocque*,' Mr Howard smiled. 'That is an ancient standing stone in Guernsey only a mile or so from our house, which is also named after it.' He shook his head. 'The elegant woman can only be your mother. My wife. I have sent for her and she should be landing at Ventnor this very evening.'

'I would like to see her,' I said.

'We will ride along in half an hour or so,' Mr Howard said. '*Les Hanois* is due on the tide.'

'My ship!' Charles said. 'I wish to show her to Sarah.'

'You love her more than life itself,' Mr Howard said.

'I do,' Charles said, and he was looking at me in the most peculiar manner.

I noticed Mr Howard's expression as he looked from Charles to me and back again.

'So, Charles, you were washed ashore and have been hiding in Wight all the time and nobody thought to tell me; well well.'

'I did not know who you were,' I reminded. 'For all I knew you wanted to kill Charles, or take him over to France to join the army or put him in prison.'

Mr Howard nodded and ran his gaze down me from the top of my head to the tips of my toes. Once more I knew that I was being scrutinised. I prepared to rebuff any plans Mr Howard had to seduce me; I had enough of that sort of thing from Captain Chadwick. Indeed, I thought, the sooner that Mrs Howard arrived on that boat the better I would like it.

'How about the French?' Mr Bertram asked. 'That was an unexpected surprise.'

'Not so unexpected, perhaps' Mr Howard said. 'They have been threatening a raid for some time. We knew they do not have the resources for a full scale invasion, although they are building up barges in all the ports on their side of the Channel. This raid was merely to test our defences, and spread alarm and despondency among our population.'

I thought of Captain Nash and James Buckett. I could not imagine men such as them being alarmed or despondent at anything the French may do.

'It did not work,' I said.

Mr Howard shook his head. 'We have been preparing for it. Our people in France sent us notice that it might happen soon so I had the Volunteers pretend to scour the fields for smugglers and Frenchmen while they were learning the lie of the land in case the French came, and I had a regiment of regulars based here before they are sent off to the West Indies.'

'You had?' I said. 'You are an important man, Mr Howard.'

He shrugged in the French fashion. 'I hope to live here soon,' he said. 'I have bought Limestone Manor. My people in France notified us that the French would pick on it as it was imposing and deserted.'

'And I brought poor Charles right into their arms,' I said.

'It was not your fault,' Charles said, 'and anyway, it all came right in the end.'

'I will be happy when Charles memory returns,' Mr Howard said, and stopped. 'Well, we will see what transpires once that happens.' He looked at his son, and then at me. I wondered if he guessed that we had been lovers. I did not care if he did.

'Shall we go?' Mr Bertram said. 'There is a fair wind from France this evening so *Les Hanois* may be in at any minute.'

It is only a few miles along the coast road to Ventnor and it was still light when we arrived. The place was in a buzz after the recent attempted invasion, with Mr Howard and the Volunteers the toast of the inhabitants. I saw Captain Chadwick in deep conversation with a blonde beauty and wondered if she was in line for his next bigamous wife, and then Kitty appeared with her smile wider than the Channel and her eyes bright with friendship.

'Sarah!' Her embrace was as warm as anything we had shared before. 'Come and meet my new beau. He is a lovely young man...'

'I can't Kitty,' I said. 'We are waiting for Charles' mother to arrive.'

'Oh my Lord! Has Charles got a mother?' Kitty looked over to Charles with her eyes wide, then, suddenly realising what she had said, she put an elegantly gloved hand to her mouth. 'My, am I not the silly one! Of course he has a mother. What I meant was: has he remembered who his mother is?'

'Mr Howard is his father,' I hissed, and then Charles joined us with smiles for Kitty and an anxious look out to sea.

As always there was a plethora of sails visible; I had thought that the French scare might have put people off travelling but it seemed that the reverse was correct. There must have been twenty five vessels in view, from lug-sailed fishing craft to one large three-master that was either an Indiaman or a Greenland ship homeward bound for London. Not that it mattered for Charles only had eyes for one vessel. He actually snatched a spy-glass from his father's hands in his eagerness to examine her.

'Look,' he pointed her out to me, while refusing to relinquish hold of his spy-glass or even lower it from his eye. 'Is she not a beauty?'

Of course all I could see was a pyramid of sails and a speck beneath, but I agreed anyway. One must, you know, if one seeks to keep the peace with one's man.

As *Les Hanois* came closer, I could see that she was indeed a beautiful vessel. Sloop rigged, she sailed with a bone between her teeth and her sails bulging under the same southerly wind that slapped the waves against the harbour wall and showered us with periodical splatters of spray.

'Your mother is in the bows,' Mr Howard had managed to borrow or steal another spy-glass from somebody.

'Oh!' I heard Charles exclamation. 'Oh! I know that woman.'

I also knew that woman. It was the same elegant woman I had seen in Limestone Manor. She was standing right at the figurehead of a naked Venus and of the two she was by far the more beautiful and more elegant. She stepped ashore with that same grace I had noted all these weeks before and Mr Howard was first to greet her.

I watched them embrace. I watched Mr Howard tell her something and she straightened up as if struck and literally marched toward us as Charles ran forward to meet her.

I could not hide my smile as mother embraced son and son embraced mother in as touching a reunion as any I have ever seen.

'Mother,' I heard Charles' voice even above the hubbub of the harbour and the call of circling seagulls. 'Come and meet Sarah, the woman that I wish to marry.'

Mrs Howard's eyes sought out mine through that crowded harbour. They were as green as her sons, calm and very serene. She nodded to me, only once, and then she smiled. I knew that everything would be all right, unless the curse did not strike as it had on my previous two wedding attempts.

So that brings us back to the scene with which I opened this account, when Kitty and I were hurrying down to the chapel at Knighton Hazard. If you remember I had recounted my words on that occasion:

'I had an idea that may remove the ill luck from my weddings,' I said, blithely aware that I was further stretching Kitty's inquisitiveness. It is a well-known say-

ing that curiosity killed the Kitty. Well, I had no intentions of ending poor Kitty's life, but I had no qualms about torturing her imagination.

'So tell me!' She stamped her foot in irritation which, you may imagine, pleased me no end.

'I shall take them down!' I announced, as if I had discovered a way of ending Bonaparte's threat to the world once and for all. 'And that will put an end to it.'

'You shall take what down?' Kitty wailed in utter frustration, and so I told her.

I had no intention of ruining my third wedding in the year, so I determined to take no chances. Anything that may act against me would be removed. I stormed into the chapel full of resolution and passion and stared about me at the beautiful room. It was redolent with poignant memories as I studied the stained glass windows and the small door through which the vicar had walked. I stepped forward and ran my hand over the altar that came from some pagan Roman site but which I had been assured would not do any harm to a Christian wedding. Other items in that room, I thought, might be less harmless.

'Mr Bertram,' I said, with one hand on my hip and the other pointing to the portraits that flanked the doorway. 'These two people, Mr and Mrs Ebenezer Bertram were the first to be married in this building; am I correct?'

'You are correct, Sarah,' Mr Bertram sounded mildly amused. 'But please remember to call me Hugo.'

I had forgotten that. 'Yes, all right, Hugo.' It seemed strange using his first name; the syllables sounded clumsy on my tongue. 'And how many other weddings have been performed in this chapel?'

Hugo Bertram pursed his lips. 'There have been about half a dozen weddings in total, including mine of course; and two of yours.'

I nodded. 'Quite so.' I pointed again to the portraits. 'You will note that the gentleman is in full hunting rig while his wife is most elegantly dressed, as if she is going to a ball? That may indicate that they are not entirely compatible with each other's life styles.'

'It may,' Hugo agreed patiently.

'Did they have a happy marriage?' I asked. 'Indeed, did their marriage last?'

Hugo shook his head. 'They had a most unhappy time together,' he said. 'Their marriage produced ten children but I believe they did not share a bedroom except to extend the family, and after the last child was born they moved to separate wings of the house. Eventually she left him to his hunting and shooting and moved to London to become the paramour of the Duke of somewhere or other.'

I nodded. 'Were the other marriages in here as unfortunate?'

Hugo pursed his lips. 'Yes they were, now you come to mention it. My father and mother used to stand in the great hall throwing insults and crockery at each other before he left for the colonies, and my wife left me for a sugar planter in Jamaica, thank God.' He shook his head. 'I pity that poor man. Let's hope that your next wedding has more success.'

'It will,' I promised, speaking more grimly than I had intended. 'I don't want these reminders of a failed marriage looking down on me. I think they put a curse on marriages here.'

Hugo looked very disappointed. 'Do you wish to be married elsewhere? I was rather looking forward to another of your weddings in my home. They are such exciting events!'

'You misunderstand me, sir,' I said. 'I have every intention of marrying here. However I have no intention of having these two faces glowering down upon me.'

'Then I shall have them moved,' Hugo said at once. 'The servants will take them down tomorrow.'

Well, as you will know by now, I am not a great hand at having others do for me what I am perfectly capable of doing for myself, so I was up the ladders within an hour and I woman- handled these portraits to the ground. They were heavier than I had imagined though, so both Hugo and Kitty had to help. Where was Charles you may ask? He was at sea, recovering his memory in his beloved boat. Or his beloved sloop, rather.

The wedding took place on Christmas Day 1803, with a fine sprinkling of snow and the chapel decorated with holly leaves, some ivy and enough mistletoe to satisfy the kissing propensities of every couple in the Back of Wight. I am a firm believer in old fashioned Christmases with greenery and carols, candles and feasting to brighten up the long dark nights.

I chose the Reverend Barwis to perform the ceremony again, partly to establish some continuity in my weddings and partly because he was reputed to be Molly's father and I liked to watch his face as Moll sat in the front pew while he preached about fidelity. Little things like that amuse me. He gave a little start as I rapped on his door and asked if he would officiate.

'You are back to the altar again then, Sarah; third time lucky I hope.'

'It will be,' I promised. 'My previous attempts were only trials.' I tried not to smile at the expression of shock on the Reverend Barwis' face.

I will not attempt to describe the wedding; you know what they are like and anyway I have already written about two of mine. There were some differences of course, as well as the lack of portraits on the wall above us. The groom was as much in love with me as I was with him, which helped a great deal, and there were no inconvenient other wives to worry about; or sudden orders for my husband to go and get himself shot by unhappy deserters. I fretted a little as I endured Reverend Barwis solemn admonitions to be faithful, tried not to smile at Molly's outburst of coughing and promised to love, honour and obey, although the last item in that list may take a little stretching from time to time.

As we gathered together after the ceremony, my mother gave Charles the obligatory mother-in-law peck on the cheek. 'Now this one is a better man for you,' she gave her approval. I am sure there was a genuine tear in her eye that time. 'I only wish that your father was here to give you away.'

'Mr Bertram, Hugo rather, did a fine job,' I said. I tried to steer the conversation onto other things, because mention of Father always made Mother sad. Luckily Mr Howard came along at that moment.

'Did you realise, Mr Howard,' I said, 'that at one time I had thought you were interested in becoming my third husband?'

'I am glad he was not,' the elegant Mrs Howard had overheard my words and glided over to say her piece. As always she made me feel like a country bumpkin with her grace and charm. 'My husband has spent the last five years of his life searching for a suitable wife for Charles. He actually sent me a long letter all about you and your friend Katherine.'

'Katherine?' I was blank for a moment. 'Oh Kitty: of course.' So that was that little mystery all cleared up. Out of curiosity, I asked, 'how did we both measure up?'

'Oh very well indeed,' Mrs Howard said. I suppose I should call her by her first name now, but you know her better by that one, so I shall continue to use it. 'Adam was quite enthusiastic about you.'

'So am I,' Charles said, proving his words with a kiss that did not need mistletoe. There was an outburst of cheering from the congregation and some copycats as well, with copy-Kitty foremost in the kissing department.

'And now to the wedding breakfast,' Hugo said, 'and let us hope for no untoward interruptions this time.'

'Perhaps we should lock the door, no?' Mrs Howard said. 'Just in case?'

Mr Howard's start was a little too natural to be an act. 'No,' he said. 'We will not do that. It is Christmas; not a day for locking anybody out of the house.'

As we entered the great hall of Knighton Hazard I found it even more elaborately decorated than on my two previous weddings, with great boughs of evergreens and enough food to feed the French, should they care to invade in friendship rather than animosity. Once again I took my place at the top table and once again I tried to quell the memories of the past events that had taken place in here.

I leaned across to Charles, 'you are not already married are you?'

'No, I am not,' he said.

'Or do you have any other surprises to spring on me?'

'No surprises at all,' he assured me.

'And you are not awaiting a call to join the army or the militia or the Volunteers?'

'I am not,' Charles assured me, smiling.

Yet even with that solemn promise my heart gave a great jump when, about half way through the meal, somebody banged with great force on the door.

'Oh Lord in Heaven,' I said, looking over to Charles. 'Here we are again.'

Reaching for my hand, he patted it in reassurance. 'It will be all right,' he said. 'You are not alone now.'

'Mrs Bembridge,' Mr Howard sounded a little strained. 'Could you answer that please?'

I thought that strange that Mr Howard should ask that in Hugo's house, particularly as Hugo was always the perfect gentleman and also employed at least a dozen servants for such tasks.

'Yes of course,' Mother said, surprisingly docile. I think everybody in the hall watched her walk past them to the great door. She struggled with the handle for a second and then threw the door wide open. Cold air carried in a blast of snow and then a man stepped into the hall.

I did not recognise him. Mother most certainly did. Her hand fluttered to her mouth. 'Oh dear God,' she said. 'Thomas, is it you?'

I half stood up in my seat as the stranger caught Mother as she fell in a complete faint. 'I am sorry I missed the ceremony, Sarah,' my father said as he smiled directly to me.

I heard Charles deep chuckle even as I held out my arms. 'How? What happened?'

'Quite simple my dear daughter,' Mr Howard said. 'Charles told me that the French may have killed or captured your father, and I had French prisoners. I found that the French still held Mr Bembridge and arranged the exchange.'

'Merry Christmas, Mother,' I said softly, knowing that she was too engrossed in her husband to hear me.

There is not much more to say in my strange little tale of how I married three husbands in the same year. In September of 1804 we called out first child Charlotte Longstone Durand. The following year we created Kitty Longstone Durand and in 1806 Adam Longstone Durand decided to join us. People have asked us if the name Longstone related to Charles' home in Guernsey. We only smile and say nothing but every year on a certain day, and often just when we feel like it, we take a night-time trip to the Longstone to verify our love for each other. I always pray for mist on such occasions, and occasionally my prayers are answered.

Oh, and I nearly forgot to add that Kitty found herself a decent husband as well, and produced an extensive litter of little Kitties. One of the prettiest has taken quite a fancy to my son, so all sorts of things may transpire in the future.

And with that I must take my leave of you.

Sarah Bembridge Durand

Limestone Manor

Isle of Wight.

July 1816.

Historical Note

There was no French raid on the Isle of Wight in 1803, although the whole of Great Britain was waiting for a French invasion. The country was filled with units of Volunteers and Militia, ready to augment the regular army if the French did manage to elude the Royal Navy and land an army in Britain.

The Long Stone does exist in Wight. It is much as described in this book, easily accessed by a footpath off the B3399, slightly to the west of Mottistone Manor. It is the only standing stone on Wight and has the alternative name of the Mottistone, which could be a Saxon name meaning 'the stone of the speakers'.

The mansions of Knighton Hazard and Limestone Manor did not exist until I transferred them from my imagination to the pages of this book. The chapel that I placed at Knighton Hazard is not situated in Wight, but it does exist. I found one similar in Duff House at Banff in Scotland, complete with the square dimensions and the twin portraits, and I thought it too good not to use. The chapel in Duff House is used for marriages and has no history of separations.

Wight was indeed the home of smugglers and fishermen at this time in its history, and smugglers often brought home French brandy, despite the two countries being at war. The law of supply and demand superseded the political legality of war.

Sarah, Kitty, Molly, Charles and even Mr Howard are all completely fictitious. I hope you enjoyed meeting them half as much as I enjoyed creating them.

Loads of love

Helen Susan Swift

Also by the Author

- Dark Mountain
- Dark Voyage
- The Handfasters
- The Malvern Mystery
- The Tweedie Passion
- A Turn of Cards
- Women of Scotland